Deadly-Go-Round

E. N. CHANTING

Cover art by Howard Artifice Book Covers

Edited by Tylee Ertel

©2025 E.N. Chanting

ISBN: 979-8-9909556-3-9 paperback

TRIGGERS: language, violent murder, and macabre death. 18+

Contents

Foreword

Dearest Enchanting Reader-

This is a fictional horror story. Although some characters may resemble historical figures, I assure you their lives in this short story are completely fictional. The idea for this story came from a particularly disturbing dream.

What would you do if you were trapped? Forced to do things that went against everything in your soul? Some of the characters in this story are faced with difficult choices and have no way out. I hope it scares and delights you.

Happy Reading!

E.N. Chanting

Dedication

Afraid to stay alone at night when it's dark?
You're stronger than you think, trust your instincts.
Sometimes we need to be thankful for the dreams that
don't come true,
they could be your worst nightmare.

In Memory of a wonderful man who will live on in our
hearts.

Chapter One

Headstrong and pouting with her headphones on, in the back seat, Rave stubbornly ignores her family's attempts to engage her. Eventually her eyes fall closed, and she blocks them out completely by falling asleep. The SUV speeds along a highway somewhere in the South, the navigation system keeps Read, the patriarch of the family, apprised of his next turn. Random, who just turned eleven, sits next to his sleeping older sister oblivious to her strife, playing his handheld game.

When Rail spots a sign for a park, she asks Read to stop so they can stretch their legs and enjoy the picnic luncheon she packed.

"And we need to walk Rogue, he's been a good boy back there but I'm sure he could use a potty break," Rail explains to Read who's used to her long-winded commentary filled with passive aggressive orders, making this exchange relatively painless.

"Are we stopping?" Random asks excitedly.

"Yes, please wake Rave so she can gather her things."

When the vehicle comes to a stop the doors open, and everyone exits with their arms full. After carrying a load of items to a picnic shelter Read collects Rogue and hooks his leash onto the harness wrapped around the friendly beast. The fluffy black K-9 is a mixed breed of sorts found at the pound. He was on his last day when the Ripley family showed up and got him pardoned from the gallows. He's very attuned to the family and he tries to anticipate their needs. As the newest member of the clan, he does a pretty good job and gets it right most of the time. The rest of the time ends with him under foot and dodging being stepped on.

The dark-haired, sullen, teen-angst-filled Rave rests her forearms on the picnic table and her chin on her hands. Unwilling or uncaring to help, she glowers while Rail hands out the carefully packaged sandwiches and little bags of chips. When a kid's juice pouch is placed in front of her, Rave has had enough. She clicks her tongue, rolls her eyes, and stomps off on her own sans sandwich. She doesn't hear her father calling after her because she dialed up the volume on her music to match her exasperation.

"Just leave her be, she's going to be sorry later when she's hungry and we don't have time to stop for her. How's your sammi, Randy?"

"It has mayo, so it's gross but I'm hungry." He takes another bite and flips his dark curls from his eyes. Rogue is happily panting beneath the table hoping for someone to be clumsy and drop some crumbs his way. He's betting on the boy, if the past holds true, since he's the most likely to share whether it's on purpose or not.

"It shouldn't be too much further to the bed and breakfast, the navigation is acting a little dodgy, but I don't think it's far off this road once we get into Hangman's Bluff. We probably have less than two hours to go," Read says to no one in particular.

"I still don't understand why you wanted to visit this dreary place. Who gives their town such an awful name? It sounds dreadful from just the name alone, though I can't wait to visit the gardens in the town square. You aren't expecting me to go to the museum, are you?" Rail asks her husband who cringes at her accusing tone.

"No. Rave and Randy can join me, or you, whichever they prefer. You can visit the greenhouse and flowers to your heart's content. I will be wrapped up in train history and the ghost tour all day. I think you'll like where we're staying, despite the name. Their website said the Hangman's Inn is a historical location. It was originally the courthouse for the whole county, and the pictures showed a garden filled with Roses and Clematis vines." He tries to offer his persnickety wife something to chew on other than his ear.

"Fine. I'll try to overlook the gruesome name. Come on Randy, let's use the restroom before we get back on the road. Read, you go wrangle Rave, she needs to use the facilities here, so we don't have to make any more stops. If there's truly a decent garden at the inn, I'd like to see it before dark."

The brow beaten man collects the family's trash and takes Rogue to look for Rave as he dumps the remains of their lunch in the bin. Rave is on a bench overlooking a stream with her headphones resting like a crown, oblivious to her surroundings. Read has heard his wife hound the girl about being safety conscious while listening to her music, he understands why his daughter is frustrated with her mother. He's frustrated with her too, but what are his options? Divorce? Nope, not for him, not after growing up with divorced parents who shuffled him back and forth using him as a pawn in their mutual hatred. He sighs and taps Rave on the shoulder.

She jolts and rips off her head gear, "Geez, dad! Don't sneak up on me like that!"

"Your mother wants you to use the restroom so we can get back on the road. We aren't stopping again."

She makes an exasperated sound, hooks her headphones around her neck, and stomps off towards the building marked, *Restroom*. Read offers the sweet dog some water and then takes him into the men's room. Random is just coming out of a stall.

"I'll take him after I wash my hands."

"Thanks. See if you can get him to pee one more time, maybe if you walk him by the tree where he already went, he'll go again."

Random dries his hands with a paper towel from the stack on the sink and takes the leash from his father.

Once they're all seated in the car and buckled up, they get back onto Route Thirteen and continue Northwest over the low hills and winding asphalt. Some of the leaves are beginning to turn yellow and a few have fallen across the road. The sun dips behind the trees and the road is darkened with shadows. Read has a feeling of foreboding rippling along his spine, and he brushes it off ignoring his instincts as they desperately try to warn him. What could possibly be wrong with a quaint bed and breakfast in the beautiful foothills of the biggest mountains in the South?

Hoping he won't find out the answer to that question, Read focuses on the road while Rail enjoys the scenery. A river follows along the road and the woods look like a fairytale painted with the bright colors of fall leaves. They only see a few scattered houses and none of them look occupied. They all seem to have that vacant look a property gets when no one has been there for an extended amount of time.

After what feels like forever to Rave, they finally pass a sign announcing they've arrived in *Hangman's Bluff, The Friendliest Town in the South.* Out of the corner of her eye, she sees a shadow shift behind a tree as they drive by. It looked like a person, but not, he was too tall and too bent. Or maybe he was wearing a strange tall hat? She shakes it off as her imagination but it's difficult to swallow as she continues to watch the woods with a chill in her chest.

Random squirms in his seat next to her and Rogue whines under his breath. She turned off her music when they passed the sign marking the town limits in hopes they were finally going to stop at their destination. But so far there's no evidence of a town, just endless woods.

"How much farther is it?"

"I don't know. The navigation isn't working right. It keeps wanting me to turn around, but it says our turn off is in three miles. Watch for *Hanging Dog Road.*"

"What on Earth is wrong with these people? Why are they so fascinated with hanging things?" Rail complains with the rhetorical question.

"It's probably a joke. You know, since the town is Hangman's Bluff, why not lean into it and mark some other things with equally gruesome names making it funny instead of spooky?"

"Hmpf. Well, the gardens better be as nice as advertised or I'm going to be very disappointed."

"Do we have our own rooms, Dad?" Random asks, hopefully.

"Yes and no. You and Rave have adjoining rooms, and you share a bathroom between you. Mom and I are across the hall, it's not a big place so I don't think there will be more than two or three other families staying there."

Rave asks, "Is there a mall anywhere around here?"

"Sorry. But there's a downtown market center. It says there's an array of small shops all around the town square. There's an art gallery, a book shop, and an antique store."

Not willing to reveal any excitement to her parents, Rave answers with one word, "Cool."

Rail calls out, "There's the turn."

The road narrows as he turns onto a lesser maintained track. They move away from the river and into the woods. As they come up over a rise, the forest begins to thin out and they're surrounded by some green pastures containing horses and cows. A farmhouse and barn dots almost every penned in property.

Finally Read spots an old wooden sign dangling from just one hook, the other having rusted away leaving the sign askew. It says, *Hang Blu In* on the part he can see. He navigates the narrow turn and climbs uphill to the ancient, blue-roofed, Victorian structure perched at the peak. As they pull into the circular drive, in front of the entrance, the house seems to loom over them. It's four stories with lots of windows, dormers, chimneys, and extravagant architectural features which would be charming on any other building. The siding is a faded gray and the shutters are blue matching the high peaked roof. The front door is a deep crimson, it looks like the entrance to hell. A chimney graces each side of the edifice promising a warm fire in multiple rooms, Read hopes their room will be appointed with such a feature.

"Okay everyone, we're here. Let's grab everything and see if we can do this in one trip."

Chapter Two

The family pushes through the heavy red portal loaded with all of their luggage. Read leaves his bags near the front door. The rest of the family dumps their items with his and enters the open front room. It looks like a Victorian parlor from the damask wall coverings to the velvet clad torturously straight-backed furniture. Rave and Randy investigate the room, afraid to sit or touch anything.

The lamps are dressed in dangling crystals and hand painted porcelain shades. Rail has never seen so many doilies in her life, every surface in the room is covered in white crocheted fabric. It feels like a cross between painfully formal and a house of ill repute. Rave likes it. Randy desperately wants to touch an ancient model airplane resting on a shelf in the dark wood apothecary cabinet nestled on the far side of the large room. The ceilings are high, and heavy drapes hang from the top of the crown molding all the way to the hand-stained hardwood floors below on either side of the blurry windows.

Read approaches what appears to be an old banker's counter. It has a variety of cubbies, drawers, and cabinet doors. There's a bell resting on top of the makeshift hotel style desk and he taps it with his finger causing the sound to ring out, startling Rave.

"Hello folks! How can I help y'all?" An average looking man of average height and build asks as he approaches from an arched doorway behind the counter.

"I'm Read Ripley, we have a reservation." The man looks over his glasses at the rest of the family mulling around the front room.

"I see. Yes, here you are, Ripley. Party of four, two rooms one of them adjoining, five nights," he states as he consults a large register sprawled on the desk.

"That's us, and a dog."

"Hmmm, ah yes, and a dog. I see you paid in full online, I'll need your identification, and a credit card for incidentals."

"Are you going to charge something on my card?"

"Not unless you incur any expenses." Rave watches her father hand over his card and driver's license. She studies the man and realizes when he walks away, she can't picture what he looked like. He had muddy brown hair and he was about the same size as her father, but his features escape her. She feels her forehead and ponders if she could be coming down with something.

"All right, Mr. Ripley, just sign here, and here. I have your keys, you're at the top of the stairs, turn right when you get there and both doors on that hallway are yours."

"What time is breakfast? And would you please recommend some place close for dinner?"

The clerk slides Read's cards across the wood countertop and places two keys in front of him. Rave watches intently determined to note every feature of the average looking man.

"Breakfast service begins at seven and ends at ten. As long as you're seated by ten, we'll serve you. The dining room is through that archway." He points to the opening opposite the parlor disguised as a brothel.

"Here's a map with some restaurants, and town isn't far. If you park at the Mercantile, you can walk to any of the places listed. You're all set." He places a printed page in front of Read while he tucks away his cards, pockets the keys, and hands the page to his wife.

"Which way are the gardens on the property?" Rail asks before the man can step away.

He assesses her before answering, "There's a door to the back patio in the dining room, you can access the garden from there. Be careful, there's an angry crow that's been harassing the gardener. Good day."

Rail watches with her mouth open as the man disappears behind the desk, through the doorway and into darkness that seems to swallow him. The oddest feeling comes over her as she struggles to recall what the man looked like or his name. Did he tell them his name?

"Come on gang, grab your bags. Randy, just take your backpack and Rogue, I'll get your bag."

The family climbs the stairs and turns into their reserved hallway, when they reach the first door Read digs the keys out of his pocket. He didn't notice until now that they're ancient keys in sync with the Victorian décor. He pushes one metal key into the keyhole on the door and tries to turn it.

"Of course, it's the wrong key." He checks the door for a number and then the key, finding no marker on either. He swaps the key for the one in his pocket and tries again with success. The room is overly frilly. The twin beds are tall with little step stools to assist with the height.

"Geez dad, it looks like an old lady was trapped in here with a sewing machine. What's with all the ruffles?" Rave queries, never one to keep her opinions to herself.

"It's the style of the place, a few frills aren't going to kill you. Get unpacked and check your bathroom, make sure there's hot water and everything works. We'll get you for dinner in half an hour. Please help your brother." She rolls her eyes, and he ignores it, convinced they're going to have a wonderful family vacation even if he has to force it down the girl's throat.

"I hope our room isn't decorated like that. You know all those ruffles are just full of dust, my allergies will go nuts if I'm stuck sleeping in a dust factory. Why did you choose this place again?" Rail not so passively addresses her spouse.

Read works quickly to get their door opened so she can get it out of her system all at once. Whatever complaints she has about the room can be dealt with swiftly so they can move on to the enjoyable portion of the trip. He breathes a sigh of relief when the door opens upon a *smooth* room. No ruffles or frills of any kind crowd their room and he grins, thinking to himself that she'll have nothing to complain about now. His righteous smile falls as soon as she walks into the room.

"It's freezing in here. Why is it so cold, is there a thermostat? You know I'll be sick by morning if it's going to be this cold." Rail looks around and pulls back the comforter, sheets, and mattress pad checking for bed bugs.

Dropping Rogue's dog bed in the corner, Read wheels their suitcase to the bench beneath the window. Rogue bounces happily into his bed and curls up to watch the people who feed him. Read opens a door to find a generous closet, and another reveals the ensuite bath. It has two sinks in an antique vanity adorned with period appropriate mirrors, and an enormous claw foot tub takes up one corner. Thankfully, the other corner contains a shower and not even Rail could find fault with that.

After they unpack and Rail wipes every surface with sanitizer, they knock on the children's door and the family heads to town for a meal. The highly forgettable clerk was right, the Mercantile isn't far and provides ample parking. The town is mostly dog friendly, and Read wonders if that's why they're the *Friendliest Town.*

Without much effort, they locate an American Bistro with an outdoor patio that allows dogs. The waitress even brings over a water bowl for Rogue and offers him a treat. Random is completely mesmerized by the attention paid to Rogue, he finds it fascinating a restaurant would serve a dog like any customer. The dog doesn't understand why, he's just happy to have the attention, and even though he's easy going, he can be a little needy. It's why they brought him, Read worried he'd be miserable without them.

After the satisfying meal they decide to see a little more of the town. Rave agrees in hopes she can visit the bookshop. Rail wants to ask about the gardens and Read is just happy to walk Rogue. Nobody asks or cares if Randy is okay with a walk, as the youngest his thoughts and wishes are often ignored. Like Rogue, he's easy going and it doesn't bother him.

"I'm going to that shop since I skipped the gardens at the inn, I'm going to spend some money. I'll meet you back at the car in a half hour," Rail announces with a smirk and aims for the Garden Emporium across the way. Rave tries her luck after her mother walks away.

"I'm going to the book shop. I'll meet you at the car." She doesn't allow any inflection to lift the end of her sentence in question, forcing it to be a statement just like her mother's selfish decree. She holds her breath waiting for a reaction from her father.

"Go ahead, just be at the car in thirty minutes."

"Thanks dad." Suddenly overcome with gratitude and forgetting her commitment to teen angst, she leans up on her tiptoes and kisses his cheek, then takes off before he can change his mind.

"I guess it's just us guys. Where do you want to go, Randy?"

"I don't know. I'm just happy to walk with you and Rogue."

"Good man. Let's check out that park. I bet Rogue will find some good smells over there."

Rogue perks up hearing his name, wagging his tail he happily sniffs his way to the park where he can already see some squirrels in need of chasing. Read considers the town, and the people meandering around the little hub of activity, he wonders if any of them are visitors like his family or if they're locals.

As he and Random walk Rogue along the winding path through the park, it follows the edge of a large pond and has a few ducks floating on its surface. Rogue barks at the feathered creatures and they choose to fly to the far end, away from his joyful invitation to play. While Read watches them take flight, he notices a ripple in the water, a rather large disturbance in the otherwise smooth reflection of the sky.

"Did you see that?"

"See what?" Randy searches for something out of the ordinary.

"There's something in the water. It was big."

"What kind of something?" Randy questions focusing on the central feature of the park.

They leave the path and approach the shoreline. Rogue sniffs at the liquid and chances a lick with his long tongue. He laps at the opaque water and splashes one foot into the pond in his excitement. A ripple projects out from his paw across the surface in a dissipating wave.

Read catches another movement from the corner of his eye.

"There!" he points. "Did you see something move?"

"I don't see anything, dad."

They both scan the pond looking for movement. Read spots another ripple near the ducks.

"By the ducks, watch for something to move over there, I just saw it."

"Oh! Yeah, I saw something!"

They remain poised watching for another disturbance on the surface, hoping to catch a glimpse of the large animal causing the movements. When nothing happens for several moments, Randy spots a chipmunk and gets distracted. Rogue is already sniffing the trail of something near the path disappearing into the woods. They let Rogue lead the way and continue on their walk. Without them to witness, a duck is pulled under by a strange blue tentacle, never to be seen again.

Chapter Three

"Come on! Hurry up, I'm hungry."

"I'll be out in a minute, quit bugging me."

When there's a knock on their door Random calls to his sister, "They're here. You're going to miss breakfast!"

"Good! Go away!"

Randy opens the door for his mother.

"Good morning, where's Rave?"

"In the bathroom, she's been in there forever." He points to the locked door across the room with his eyes rolled up.

"All right. She can find us in the dining room when she's finished. Let's go down for breakfast. Did you sleep okay?"

"I guess. I had some weird dreams, and I kept hearing a weird rattling sound. Did you hear it?"

"I'm not sure I know what you mean by a rattling noise. Was it in your room or outside the door?"

"It was in my room, like chains banging into each other. I think it was in the vent over my bed."

"Show your father after breakfast, he can complain to the manager if it's something they need to fix. I'm going to the botanical garden today, are you going with me?"

"Sorry, Mom, I want to check out the trains with Dad."

"It's okay, I figured you'd prefer the trains. Something sure smells good, let's sit here, dad should be right down."

As Rail and Randy take a seat at a large table another pair sits at a small table opposite them. It's an older couple who looks ready to do some damage at the discount market. They nod at Rail and Randy in greeting and Rail smiles at them in return. Read enters the room and joins them just when the waitress arrives with juice and coffee.

She passes out the coffee to the adults and juice for Random. "Can I get you anything else to drink?"

"May I please have some water?" Randy asks politely.

"You sure can. I think the cook is making some pancakes, if you want, she doesn't mind if kids want to watch, you'll get to be an official taste-tester."

"Can I, Mom?" Randy asks, looking at his tougher parent with pleading eyes and his hands pressed together for good measure.

"Sure. Don't go anywhere but the kitchen."

"I promise."

"Come on kiddo, I'll show you where," the waitress, with Tiffany on her nametag offers. Randy hops from his seat and follows her from the room.

"I hope he doesn't have too much sugar being a taste-tester. Should we bring a pancake back for Rogue?"

"No. He seemed like he had a bit of an upset stomach when I walked him this morning. He kept wanting to eat grass."

"Yuck. I'm glad he didn't vomit in our room."

"Me too. I didn't think to bring anything to clean with if he had an accident or any other messes came up. Are you excited to go to the gardens today?"

"I'm so excited. I read online that they have a rare orchid greenhouse. I'm excited to see what they have in there. How about you, excited about your trains?"

"Yes. They have a special tour today that allows us to take a short ride in the refurbished dining car from the original Shooting Star Line, it's a ghost tour. Randy and I will have lunch there. Do you know if Rave is coming with me?"

"She hasn't said, but I'm certain she's not interested in coming with me. Speak of the devil, there she is, our sweet child," Rail adds the last part under her breath with a hint of sarcasm.

"Where's Randy?" Rave questions.

"He went into the kitchen for pancakes," Read answers with a smile.

"There are pancakes?"

"Apparently, why don't you go find him in the kitchen? He went through that archway." Rail points in the direction she last saw Random.

"Okay."

Rave passes through the archway and can hear kitchen sounds at the end of the hall, she follows the sounds and the delicious smell of bacon and maple. When she enters the kitchen, she's surprised to find Random seated at a two-place round table with a plate of chocolate chip pancakes stacked four high. Her mouth waters.

"Hello? I'm Rave, Randy's sister. May I please have some pancakes too?"

The gray haired and slightly hunched woman turns and looks her over, "You sure can. Have a seat with your brother and I'll fix you right up." The elderly woman chooses a plate from a pile of them and starts flipping pancakes onto it. When she has a good tall stack, she places it in front of Rave, then pushes the syrup toward her.

Rave douses the flat cakes with more sugary liquid than necessary and immediately carves out a chunk shoving the forkful into her mouth.

"Mmmm, vis if fo good!" She mangles her compliment through a mouthful.

"What's this?" Randy asks. He plays with the trim along the edge of the table, flipping up the small photos lined there.

"That... is a Deadly-Go-Round," the cook answers cryptically.

"What's a dead round?" Rave asks, curious now, looking at the faded photos along the edge of the table on her side.

"Deadly-Go-Round. It's like a roulette wheel; it spins and then it stops on a photo with the spinner's assignment lined up with that arrow on top. It's an antique. It was here when the owner bought the place, so we don't know much about it beyond what it's called and how it spins."

"Who are these people in the photos?"

"Those are criminals, murderers, serial killers, the worst of the worst. Pretty much anyone you land on will be guaranteed to be the scariest monster you'd never want to meet."

"Why do they spin? What do you mean, your assignment?"

"Legend has it, if you spin the Deadly-Go-Round whoever it stops on becomes your assignment to kill. If you don't kill them, you can't leave town and eventually they'll kill you, you know if you don't kill them first."

Tiffany buts in, "Elvira! Don't scare them with your silly tales. Let them eat in peace. Kids don't listen to her, she's just trying to scare you because she thinks it's funny. Hurry up and finish your pancakes, your parents will have their food in a minute. Do you want anything else, in addition to the pancakes?"

Randy makes a request for bacon, but Rave is mesmerized by the faces along the edge of the table. She touches each one and looks them over, most of them appear to be mug shots taken when they were arrested, but a few look like they're free and living a normal life. She pushes the edge of the table where the photos attach and moves it back and forth testing how it would spin.

"I don't think you should spin it, what if what Elvira said is true? What if you have to kill the person in the photo to leave town?" Random whispers with trepidation.

"Don't be ridiculous. Obviously, that's not possible, she was just trying to scare you, she probably gets her kicks scaring children."

"It worked. I don't like this weird table, it creeps me out."

"Then maybe you shouldn't watch while I spin it." Rave pulls back on the spinning edge and then pushes it forward, so it gets a good spin. There's a rattling sound as it spins, but the mechanism moves smoothly spinning much faster and longer than Rave expected. When it comes to a stop, she spots the arrow shaped like a diamond pointed at the photos and her arrow is lined up with a photo of a red-haired woman. She lifts the photo on its hinge that's attached to the spinning ring for a better look at the image. She realizes the photo can fold all the way up onto the table so she can read the back of it.

"Sarah Jane Robinson, known as the Boston Borgia, 8-11 victims by poisoning. Caught August 12, 1886, sentenced to death, commuted to life in prison."

"This says she killed 8-11 victims. Freeeeeaky," Rave says in the voice of a cartoon ghost.

"You shouldn't have done that, what if Elvira was telling the truth?" Random whispers to Rave trying not to catch the attention of the old woman working at the stove.

But he didn't need to worry about capturing her attention, she already knew what Rave did, and she had a large, evil smile on her face. She waits patiently for Random to make his spin, she knows he will, they always do. No matter how scared they say they are, nobody can resist the call of the Deadly-Go-Round.

"You should try it. I think it's cool. Maybe you'll land on someone interesting too," Rave tries to entice her brother.

"Nope. I don't even want to touch it. I don't like the rattling noise it makes when it spins. Last night while I was trying to sleep, I heard that same sound."

"It couldn't have been this table. Our room is on the other side of the inn. It's okay if you're chicken, you're just a little kid. Lots of little kids are scared of everything. Even a ridiculous story would be scary for most little kids. Come on, are you done? Let's find Mom and Dad."

"I'm not a chicken. I just don't think we should be doing something we were told not to do."

"A chicken says what?"

"What?"

"See, you're chicken. I told you, it's fine if you're not brave enough, you're still a little kid."

"I'm not that much younger than you, and I'm not chicken." Trying to look brave and more grown than he is, Random puts his hand on the spinning edge of the table and pulls it back before pushing it around the same way his sister did. When he lets go it spins fast, the photos lift from the centrifugal force from the speed. As the ring of photos slows, they fall back down and the diamond arrow on Random's side of the table points to a photo.

He looks at the faded old image of a normal, average looking man, wearing a hat and moustache of the time period. Swallowing hard, hoping his killer isn't as scary as the one Rave landed on. He lifts the photo, tipping it up onto the table to read the back.

"H.H. Holmes, known as the Beast of Chicago. 1 confirmed victim, 9 suspected. Apprehended November 17, 1894. Hanged for his crimes May 7, 1896."

Randy sucks in a nervous breath causing Rave to ask, "What does it say?"

"He was suspected of nine murders and hanged. What do you think will happen now?"

"I think if we don't go out to meet Mom and Dad, they're going to come looking for us. Give me your plate, you get our cups, let's take these to the sink."

Randy collects their cups and looks over his shoulder at the odd table one last time before following her to the sink. She rinses their dishes and places them in the sink to be washed in the dishwasher. They dry their hands and before they leave the room, Rave calls out to the chef.

"Thank you for the pancakes."

"Oh, you're quite welcome. It was my pleasure." Rave frowns as the old woman chuckles under her breath. What's funny? She wonders as she directs her little brother to the dining room where their parents are finishing up.

"How were the pancakes?" Read asks with a huge smile knowing both children have an affinity for the overly sweet breakfast treats.

"They were good," Rave answers without elaborating.

"How were yours, buddy?"

"Good." Random can't bring himself to say more when what feels like an ever-tightening strand of barbed wire is wrapped around his middle, making him feel distracted and nervous.

"You feeling alright sweetie?" Rail asks, noticing Randy is much more subdued than usual, especially after having a big dose of sugar.

"Yeah. Can we go, Dad?" Read gulps the last of his coffee and nods.

"Are you coming with us or your mother, Rave?" The girl looks at her parents and chooses to take her chances with her mother. Even though they don't usually get along for more than five minutes at a time, Rave feels bad leaving her mother alone on vacation, guilt is a tool her mother employs often.

"I'll go with Mom." Rail smiles satisfied and pleasantly surprised, somehow Rave seems much calmer than the angry girl from last night.

"Great! Let's get going. I guess we'll meet back here at what? Five o'clock?" Rail confirms.

"Yeah, that should be plenty of time for us to have the ride and be back. All right let's get going." Read guides Randy back to their room to collect Rogue before going to the front parlor where the shuttle to the train museum will pick them up sometime in the next twenty minutes. The entire train experience is dog friendly, and Read is relieved he doesn't require the pet-sitting services offered by the inn.

Rave and Rail leave in their SUV, heading into town to get to the botanical gardens on the other side of the little metropolis. Rave is quiet and thinking about the red-haired Boston Borgia. Rail is lost in her own day-dreams about orchids. If she finds a rare orchid and can get some cuttings, she might be able to win the annual flower show back home.

Chapter Four

"Dad? Can I ask you something?" Random queries.

"Always. What's up?"

"Well, something happened at breakfast and now I'm worried about it."

"What happened?" Read asks deeply concerned.

"There's this weird table, Elvira says it's a Deadly-Go-Round, and if you spin it you have to kill the killers or you can't leave town, and I didn't want to spin it. But then Rave spun it, and she said I was a chicken if I wouldn't spin it too and I landed on a serial killer, the Beast of

Chicago and she landed on the Boston Borgia, and now we have to kill them so we can go home. But they're already dead so I don't think we can kill them. What if we can't leave because we didn't kill them? The table scares me because it makes the same rattling noise I heard in my room. This place is kinda of spooky. Do you think I'm going to get killed if I don't kill the Holmes guy?"

"Whoa! That's a lot of information. Let me ask some questions to clarify. First of all, who's Elvira?"

"She's the cook who gave me pancakes. She was nice but then she laughed about the table and Tiffany told her not to scare us."

"All right, and Tiffany is the waitress, right? What did you call this table?"

"It's a Deadly-Go-Round, it's in the kitchen and it's round with these pictures all along the edge and if you spin it the arrow lands a killer, and you have to kill them, or they'll kill you." Seeing Random visibly afraid, Read is getting angry with this Elvira person. Why would she tell a little boy about all this killer stuff?

"You said it's in the kitchen, right? Will you show me?"

"I don't want to go back in there, Dad, but I'll show you. It's super creepy." Read and Rogue follow Random to the kitchen at the end of the arched hall. Elvira is still working at the stove. There's another hour of breakfast service but with only a few guests it shouldn't be too difficult for her to keep up with orders.

"Get that beast out of my kitchen!" the elderly chef hollers at Read. He looks down and realizes he's walking into a kitchen with a dog.

He hands the leash to Random, "Hey bud, please take Rogue into the hallway and wait there for me, okay?"

"Okay, come on Rogue." The boy leads the dog into the hall and relief floods him as soon as he's able to escape the room with that horrific table.

Read approaches the woman who's sweaty and red faced from standing over a hot stove. She stirs something in a pot, and he can't identify the brown substance.

"I'm terribly sorry for bringing the dog in, I wasn't thinking. I wanted to speak to you about your scary story. It upset my son and now he's terrified he's going to die because of it. I just wanted to let you know and ask you to avoid telling him any more stories. He's quite scared of some table."

"It's not technically a table even though we use it as one but it's much more. It's a Deadly-Go-Round, it's a divination device that connects the spinner's soul with the spirit of the killer on the wheel. It connects them and requires them to kill the assigned killer before they get loose in your world and kill the spinner instead."

"That's crazy, please stop telling my son anything about it. Where is this table?" Read glances around and spots a table with a few plates on it. He moves in for a closer look and reaches out to touch the cards.

"Be careful, if you spin it, you'll need to kill the murder-er you land on too." He chuckles at how hard she's selling it. Maybe the inn is trying to get the ghost hunting crowd to stay here. He imagines it would be lucrative with how old and spooky this whole town seems to be.

He pushes a little harder on the edge trying to get a feel for how the thing works. He tries to look at the photos closest to him to see if they're anyone whose name he's heard before and he notices a tension in his stomach, Randy is right this thing is creepy. When he leans down over the table, one of the killers catching his eye, his hand slips against the spinning ring at the top edge where it meets the table. His mistaken brush against the ring sends it spinning and he marvels at how fast it spins when he barely bumped it. The cards with the killers lift again with the force of the movement. When the ring of cards slows, the diamond-shaped arrow in front of Read points to card after card until it comes to rest precisely in the middle of a card.

Read looks at the image on his card and it's a little difficult to see much more than a shape which is most definitely a human. He lifts the card seeking a better view and more information. He realizes he can flip the card onto the table and reads the back with some surprise.

"Ed Gein, also known as The Butcher of Plainfield. 2 confirmed murders, 7 more suspected, and 9 mutilated corpses from the local cemetery. Apprehended November

16, 1957. Sentenced to a maximum-security mental health facility until death July 26, 1984."

Read removes his hands from the table post haste. He's heard of this murderer and recognizes that a couple movies are loosely based on this particular serial killer. The Texas Chainsaw Massacre and Silence of the Lambs are both inspired by the disturbing behavior of this very mentally ill man.

"It won't help to stop touching it now. You've spun, you have to kill him, or you won't be able to leave, and he'll come after you."

"You know you sound crazy when you say that, right?" Read asked the obviously disturbed cook. Her eyes narrow as she evaluates him, her lips pressed together, she seems to determine him lacking.

"You can think I'm crazy, but soon enough you'll find out I'm right. My advice is to strike fast. As soon as you see him, kill him right away so he doesn't have any chance to come after you. You should probably help your kids too, make sure they act quickly, as soon as they spot theirs."

Woof! Woof! Rogue rushes into the room, his leash dragging the ground behind him and barking at the woman, he runs to the table and jumps up putting his front paws against the Deadly-Go-Round. His paws scrape against the table's surface as he continues to bark aggressively and completely out of character for the easy-going K-9.

"I'm sorry dad! He freaked out and took off pulling the leash right out of my hand."

"It's all right, just take him back out." Read moves to help Randy gather Rogue and retrieve his leash. When they get him down off the table, the ring is spinning. Rogue must've knocked it into motion with his angry barks and large paws.

When it comes to a stop, Read and Randy are joined by Rogue to see who it stopped on. Rogue almost looks like he's examining the photo of a man, he then presses his nose beneath the card and flips it up onto the table and looks at Read expectantly.

"This is crazy, did you see that?" he asks Randy.

"I told you it was weird. What does his card say?"

"Theodore Robert Bundy, also known as Ted Bundy. Victims: 20 confirmed, 30 confessed, 36+ suspected. Apprehended August 16, 1975. Executed by electric chair January 24, 1989."

Rogue sneezes. Then he pulls on the leash in Randy's hand taking him from the room. Read isn't sure what to do or say now. He eyes the old woman and takes in a deep breath to fortify himself.

"I'm leaving, we're going on the shuttle to the train museum. Please, just don't talk to Randy about this anymore. Thank you."

"Remember what I said, strike fast. Good luck to you." She turns back to the pot on the stove, and he opens his mouth to admonish her for perpetuating the ridiculous tale but closes it again with a small smacking sound. It just seems pointless to say anything else. He leaves to find his boys. Even though Read is reluctant to leave Rogue behind in the hotel, he decides to stick with the plan.

Chapter Five

When Rail and Rave park at the gardens they collect their bags to bring inside. Rave carries her phone in her pocket and a small backpack over her shoulder while Rail pulls a large tote over her own shoulder. Rail's bag contains sunscreen, her wallet, phone, snacks, bottles of water, clippers, some small burlap bags to keep clippings, and a few other miscellaneous essentials.

They begin their self-guided tour of the gardens in a playful fountain display where adorable frogs, turtles, and otters are sculpted with human expressions and look like real life cartoon figures made from a variety of mediums.

The water is carefully timed to squirt out in a sequence that makes it look like the liquid is jumping from place to place to play a game of keep-away with the animal statues.

Rave giggles at the cute little frogs, she likes them because their legs are comically long, and their feet are Big Foot sized which leaves her delighted. Plus, green is her favorite color, and the frogs are a bright shade that makes her think of grass in the summertime in the field near her house.

Rail likes the complicated otter sculptures, their long bodies are twisted around and through obstacles making them seem like their middles are more flexible than could be possible in real life. The ladies move on to a path that leads them into a maze of roses and the flowers come in many shades including red, pink, white, yellow, and orange. In the center of the large maze is a section of rare colors such as multiple shades of purple, black, and green.

They follow the exit path into a stand of trees which is quickly replaced by bamboo and some pagoda statuary mixed with arches, bridges, and other East Asian themed décor. It's as if they've been transported to a foreign land on the other side of the Pacific Ocean, perhaps Japan. The greenery has changed into cherry trees and others she doesn't recognize beyond having seen them in Japanese gardens before. Some of the trees have thin branches that all hang down in a cascade like a waterfall of green.

"I think this is my favorite style. I want to go to Eastern Asia and see Japan, Hong Kong, Vietnam, and some of the islands nearby. It's so beautiful. I've seen some gorgeous photos of cherry trees in bloom with the ice capped mountains in the background, it makes me want to see it in person so much." Rave expresses. A dream she hopes to make come true one day.

"It is quite beautiful. I think you can do some college courses abroad, it's a great way to travel while you continue your education."

"I'm definitely interested."

Rave's mouth falls open as she watches a red-haired woman walk past and continue on ahead of her and Rail. Her mind tries to process what her eyes see. Was that? It couldn't be, she's dead. It had to be an odd coincidence since she was involved with that spinning table of death earlier, it must be her mind playing tricks.

"Are you all right?" Her mother asks.

"Yeah. I'm fine. That lady just looked familiar, and it surprised me is all. There's the greenhouse, do you want to look at the orchids now?" Rave asks, diverting their attention in the opposite direction from the woman with red hair.

As her mother oohs and aahs over the beautiful and distinctly exotic orchids, Rave can't help searching for a shock of red hair. She wants to see the woman's face again so she can reassure herself it's definitely not anyone she needs to be worried about.

By the time they're finally ready to leave the greenhouse, Rave needs the restroom and as luck would have it there's a restroom attached to the building just outside near the exit of the greenhouse. She enters and notices one stall is occupied so she chooses another one, two stalls away and lost in her thoughts she doesn't pay attention to the flush in the other stall and when she opens her door, the other occupied stall opens as well.

The woman's red hair immediately draws her attention. She examines the lady's face carefully, comparing it to the image in her mind from the photograph on the Deadly-Go-Round. This woman is a little younger but otherwise she could pass for a close relative of the Boston Borgia and this revelation causes Rave's eyes to open extra wide in surprise while she stares at the woman for an excessively rude amount of time.

"Do you need something?" the red-haired woman asks, sounding somewhat annoyed but also alarmed as if Rave might be having a medical emergency.

"No. I'm sorry. You look like someone, and I was trying to figure out if you're her. I didn't mean to be rude," Rave stumbles over her attempt to reassure the woman.

"Oh. I hate it when that happens. My friends call me Janie, what's your name?"

"Rave. Nice to meet you. Sorry, again."

"That's a cool name. Don't worry about it. Have a good day, maybe I'll see you around."

The woman has an accent Rave doesn't recognize but she seems nice enough and not serial killerish at all. Rave relaxes.

"Thanks. Yes, you too. See you." The woman exits the restroom, and Rave splashes a little water on her face then pats it dry. It helps her feel a little more present and she rejoins her mom outside.

"I'm getting hungry, how about you?" Rail asks upon her return.

Rave's stomach growls and she and her mom share a laugh. They follow the signs to the Garden Café, but when they arrive it's closed with a notice from the County Board of Health. Apparently, a former employee has come down with Hepatitis and as a precaution they've closed the restaurant until the incubation period has passed. Disappointed, the duo decides to leave the gardens and head into town for some lunch.

They park across from the train depot and decide to try out the Wrong Side of the Trax Bistro. According to the menu posted in the window it's eclectic American and French cuisine and meets Rail's requirements, with some fancy soup and salad options while still offering appetizing burgers with potatoes for Rave. When they enter the small but modern and impeccably decorated dining room they find Read and Randy seated at a table for four.

"Well, fancy meeting you here! I thought you were eating on the train, what happened?"

"The train dining car got sick so they can't serve any food," Random answers. Rail raises her brows and seeks clarification from Read with a look.

Read responds to her unasked query, "The dining car is supplied by another restaurant, and they had an employee come down with Hepatitis, so they're temporarily closed for cleaning until the incubation period passes. What are you guys doing here?"

"I think your other restaurant is the same one we tried at the Botanical Gardens. May we join you?"

Read chuckles at their shared circumstances, "Have a seat. Here comes our waitress, we just put in our order. You have good timing even if your luck is as bad as ours."

"Hi, I'm Mary, what can I offer you to drink?"

Rave speaks up, "I'll have a sweet tea, and Mom will have water with lemon. Thank you."

"Have a look at these menus and I'll be right back with your drinks."

Rail smiles, enjoying the change in Rave today. Since her teenage moods are unpredictable, her parents have learned to enjoy any good moments when they happen because they're often fleeting.

"Are you finished at the train depot then?"

"For today. How about you, are you finished at the Gardens?"

"Yeah, I'm not going back today. Let's go to the inn and collect Rogue. We can take him to that waterfall trail I found on the map at the inn. We can all get some exercise, and Rogue needs a good walk."

"Sounds great."

They order and eat a delicious meal then everyone leaves with a full belly. When they return to the inn Rogue is so excited to go for a ride in the car he runs full speed and leaps into the cargo area bouncing and wagging with joy.

It's a quick trek into the hills and the trail is up a beautiful narrow road bordered by trees and a stream. You really couldn't ask for prettier scenery. When the family parks in the lot there's only one other car parked there. It's a pale-yellow Volkswagen Beetle from the nineteen-seventies. Of course, the kids have no clue about a car that old but Read and Rail have memories of seeing a few of them in their youth. There aren't many around anymore. Read's father had photos of the one he had in high school, and it was old way back then. Read admires the car for a few extra moments before the rest of his clan urges him onto the trail excited to see the waterfall.

Rogue leads them by pulling hard on his lead, but not hard enough to cause Read to lose his footing. The trail makes a gradual climb, and it doesn't take the wind out of anyone but Rogue. He's panting and wagging the entire way to the waterfall.

When the family reaches the pinnacle, the view is stunning. They didn't encounter any other hikers on their way up, but a young man and an even younger girl are at the railing admiring the eighty-seven-foot-high waterfall and snapping photos. When the family starts taking pictures with their phones the young man smiles and offers to take a family photo for them. Rail hands over her phone and instructs her family to pose and 'say cheese.' The young man takes a few for them since Rogue wasn't one hundred percent cooperative.

"He's a nice pup. What's his name?" the young man asks.

Rave answers, "That's Rogue. We got him from the pound, so we don't know what type of dog he is."

The young man kneels to pet Rogue and offers his opinion, "I think he has some type of herding dog in him, maybe a Border Collie or Australian Shepherd. He sure is a nice fellow. Huh, boy? You like your ear scratched, don't you?"

Rail is satisfied with the family portraits after examining them. She stands beside Rave and smiles at the handsome stranger just now noticing his good looks and wavy brown hair.

"Thanks so much for taking those pictures. Would you like me to take one of you and your...friend?"

"Oh, uh, no thanks. We already took a bunch of selfies, we're all set. Sorry, where are my manners? I'm Theo and my friend is Kimmy." He holds his hand out to shake with Rail who obliges. Next, he offers his hand to Rave, and she shivers at his touch, something about him creeps her out and she scans his face, noting the strong jaw and pleasant dimples. She concludes there's something not right about him despite his good looks and steps away to avoid touching him again.

Read steps up keeping a tight rein on Rogue, to meet the helpful young man, "Hi, I'm Read. Is that your Bug in the parking lot?"

Theo smiles, "It sure is, I've had it forever. She's a beauty for a relic, right?"

"Yeah. My dad had one when he was in high school, and it was old then. Yours looks like you just drove it off the assembly line. Did you restore her yourself?"

"I'm the only one who's touched her. You have to be patient and really enjoy your work, you know?" Theo smiles and his eyes travel to Rave in a way that makes her want to vomit. She joins Randy at the railing turning her back on the creepy man.

"I get it. Enjoy your day, we're going to scope out the scenery for a bit."

"Well, it was a pleasure meeting you, I'm sure I'll see you around. Enjoy the rest of your day. Come on Kimmy, time to go." Rail gets an unpleasant feeling in her stomach as Theo guides Kimmy away with his fingers clasped to the back of her neck. It's as if he's forcing her to go with him and Rail's hair stands on end even as she raises her hand in farewell to the pair. Rogue whines and pulls against his harness wanting to follow them as they vanish around a corner and out of sight.

Read still has a smile on his face from the interaction, "He was nice. He seemed familiar somehow though. Did he look like someone famous?"

"Maybe. Come on, let's see where the trail continues, maybe we can get closer to the falls," Rail answers, shaking off the unease brought on by the too handsome and exaggeratedly polite stranger.

Chapter Six

B ack at the hotel, showered and resting, Rail asks, "So you're saying the kids both spun this antique table thing and now they have to worry about some kind of serial killers? Why would anyone have a table like that in their kitchen?"

"No. Yes. Not exactly. We all spun it, the lady in the kitchen, the chef I guess, said when the table lands on a serial killer whoever spun it has to kill that serial killer, or they can't leave. But it's just a table, an antique with an urban legend attached. It's not real. Like that kids game,

Bloody Mary. If you say it three times she doesn't actually show up and kill you."

"Tell that to Tamarah Monet Marx."

"Who's Tamarah Monet Marx?"

"She was a girl from middle school. She spent the night at her grandmother's house and stood in front of the mirror, said that name three times, and nobody ever saw her again."

Read laughs, "What? You're joking, right? She just moved away or something and that was just a rumor someone started."

"No. Her cousin said she disappeared and none of us ever saw her again. I refuse to ever say that name just in case." Her eyes are wide, and her jaw is set.

"Come on. You know that's ridiculous. Sit with me and I'll protect you." He pulls her close and she reluctantly snuggles under his arm while goosebumps cover her own arms. Read kisses her temple and then he kisses her cheek.

When his lips reach her ear, she pulls away and turns on him, "We don't have time right now. We have to get the kids for dinner, get up."

With disappointment written across his face Read exits the bed and collects his shoes, bringing them to the chair to put them on. Rogue recognizes the connection between shoes going on feet and him going outside. He pulls his harness and leash from the end of the bed and brings it to Read, sitting almost patiently in front of him.

Rail slips on her own shoes and swipes some pale lipstick across her lips. Then she checks her hair in the mirror and looks behind her reflection with trepidation, having been reminded of the demise of her childhood friend, Tamara, her fear of things lurking in a mirror returns with a vengeance. She clears her throat and has a stern inner conversation about childish fears. Then she straightens her shoulders and lifts her chin in defiance against any and all childhood fears.

After retrieving the children, the family, canine included, heads to town for a meal. This time they opt for an Italian restaurant with tables under a large awning outside allowing Rogue to join them. They all have some form of pasta and protein except Random who chooses a personal sausage and pepperoni pizza. His mother doesn't usually approve of pizza, but the vacation relaxes her usual rules, and Randy isn't going to miss out on the chance for pizza outside of his school cafeteria. Rogue is pleased with the serving of noodles and a few bland doggie meatballs.

When they're finished with a shared tiramisu, the group let's Rave lead them to the book shop. The store is also dog friendly, and they even have little dog sofas in each circle of chairs grouped as a reading area. Rave is impressed with their collection of fantasy books, and she perused the section looking at each cover and reading the blurbs on the backs of the books, she chooses two she can't live without.

Rail investigates the gardening section while Read and Randy look at the selection of robotics instructional manuals. Rogue is happily sniffing every surface and cataloguing the smells of other dogs who've roamed these hallowed aisles. He's a good boy and doesn't lift his leg even though he desperately wants to tell the other dogs he was here.

He marks the outside brick wall as soon as his family exits the shop. Rave carries a bag with two books about a far-off place filled with werewolves and vampires. Rail clutches a book about the most rare and exotic orchids, while Randy holds a large bag with an illustrated book of Robots you can Make at Home. Everyone is happy, especially Rogue now that he's finally been able to leave his scent for the other dogs in town.

The family returns to the inn and passes through the entry, past the gaudy parlor, Rave and Randy take Rogue and rush up the stairs eager to start reading. Rail walks toward the dining room and Read follows absently.

"Do you think they'll have some tea in the kitchen?"

"The clerk said something about beverages when he showed us to our room, but I can't remember what he said. It won't hurt to ask."

They enter the kitchen and find Elvira kneading bread dough on the long metal prep counter. She looks up when they enter and smiles to herself.

"Evening folks, how can I help ya?"

"Do you have any chamomile tea? I ate too much and I'm afraid I'll be up all night regretting it."

"Sure. Let me put the kettle on." She fills the metal tea kettle and places it on the front burner which she lights with a twist of the knob. Then she reaches up into a cupboard and retrieves a cup and saucer placing it in front of Rail.

"The tea is in that box, help yourself." She points to an antique tea caddy. Rail opens the lid and reads the packets until she finds a few bags of the tea she wants. She takes two, she hates weak tea. The kettle whistles and Elvira pours the steaming liquid into the cup where Rail placed the bags and she sets a spoon next to the saucer.

"Thank you so much."

"My pleasure, Miss. Would you like cream, honey, or lemon?"

"Just a spot of cream and honey would be perfect." Rail notices Read looking at the round table against the wall. Her skin pebbles with goosebumps as she recalls what he told her earlier about that particular antique table.

"Here you are, please have a seat," Elvira indicates towards the strange table. Rail accepts her offer and carefully pulls out a chair. As she sits, Read joins her in the other seat.

Rail pours the cream and honey into her cup, stirring gently. She looks at the edge of the table and clearly sees the photos of serial killers lined up there. She sees people indiscriminately placed in no obvious order.

"Thank you. It's Elvira, right?"

"Yes ma'am, you're welcome."

"May I ask you something?"

"Of course, Miss."

"My children told me something odd about this table. I wondered if you would please tell me about it." Elvira looks at Read, she told him too, but she chooses to indulge his wife.

"Yes, Miss. That's a Deadly-Go-Round. When you spin it, the table chooses a photo, and you must kill the person in that picture before you'll be allowed to leave. It's an antique with a bit of a dark history."

"Who made such a thing? Why would anyone make such a terrible piece of furniture?"

"That... I can't say. I imagine someone had a reason. There's a legend it was the devil himself, and he uses it to torture his most evil guests. They have to die again and again. But if you ask me, it seems he's corrupting those he makes do the killing, making more killers to add to his collection."

"Hmm. That all sounds so untoward, why is this awful table in the kitchen?"

"Ah, that's the question, isn't it? My uncle used to own this place and when he got too old, I took over. But, before he passed, he made me promise to keep it exactly as it is, he didn't even want me to change the paint color. I've since realized the place probably wouldn't allow it anyway. Too much history in these walls, you can't fight that."

"I suppose not. Thank you, Elvira. This tea hit the spot. I feel sleepy already. Let's go upstairs, honey."

Read stands and holds out a hand to Rail which she carefully accepts. She carries her cup and spoon to the sink before joining Read and turning for the dining room.

"Good night, Elvira."

"Good night, Miss and Mister."

After a good night's rest, probably thanks to the tea, Rail wakes feeling refreshed and silly for worrying about childhood fears. The family gathers for breakfast in the dining room and when Random asks if he can have pancakes in the kitchen again, both his parents and his sister all quickly respond with a stern, 'no!' With his easy disposition, Random doesn't push and opts for the bacon and eggs with an English muffin.

When they're all full and planning out their day Rave asks, "Would it be all right if I stayed in town? I want to hang out at the bookshop and finish my book. I can get a sandwich from the kitchen to bring with me. Please?"

Read looks to Rail, allowing her to make most of the parenting decisions keeps him from fighting with his wife more often. He's usually at work anyway, where she's home with them most of the time and privy to their schedules and necessities. In fact, if anyone ever asked him the secret to a happy marriage, he would answer, let her make the house and child rearing decisions. Luckily, nobody ever asks.

"All right, with rules. You can't leave the bookshop. Is your phone fully charged?"

"Yeah, and I'll have my charger, so it stays that way."

"You need to put the inn address and phone number into your phone. Do you have Aunt Liz's number in case of emergency?"

"Yes. Thank you. You're the best mom ever."

"Yeah well, I'm trusting you with a lot, don't break my trust or it will never happen again."

As they stand, finished with breakfast, Rave hugs her mother and her father in an uncharacteristic display of affection. They both soak in the rare event. As a family, they collect Rogue to take him for a final walk before heading out for their chosen activities. Random chooses to join his father once again, but Rail doesn't mind. Without any children she can focus on the orchids for as long as she likes without distractions.

When they enter the lobby, a new guest is checking in and he has a small black Scottish Terrier. As soon as the little fellow spots Rogue he begins barking and pulls away from his master who wasn't paying attention and had let his grip on the leash relax while he was shuffling credit cards and ID in his wallet for the check-in process. When the squat little dog charges past Rogue he gives chase, yanking Randy behind him.

The Scottie runs directly to the kitchen and hides beneath the dreaded table of death. Rogue follows, knocking over a plant in the dining room and then a chair at the little divining table. When the chair falls it knocks against the edge of the Deadly-Go-Round, sending it spinning fast. Rail was the quickest to respond to the emergency situation of their runaway dog and she followed as fast as she could into the kitchen. She doesn't even notice the table has been sent spinning as she grabs for Rogue's leash. He's barking wildly at the little Scottish beast, and he fights against the restraint now being pulled tight around him.

When the dust finally settles, Rogue has two paws on a chair and Rail has one palm flat against the antique surface of the killer table. The spinning stops and the diamond shaped indicator points to a photo on Rail's side of the table. Everyone freezes as they realize how they've ended up. Even Rogue looks frozen with concern. The owner of the little dog pulls him from beneath the table and apologizes with a heavy accent as he leaves the room.

Elvira approaches the family, "Well, Missus, it seems you and the dog have made your assignment. That's all of you."

"What the hell does that mean?" Read asks exasperated.

"It means it begins now. You might want to stick together, for safety's sake. Your sandwiches are ready, young miss." Elvira casually hands a paper sack to Rave as the family remains stuck processing the extent of their circumstances.

"What do I do now?" Rail asks.

With wide and fearful eyes Randy speaks first, "You flip it over and see who you've got." He reaches out and flips over the photo lined up with Rail's arrow. He scans the information and swallows hard.

Rail reads the words on the back of the photo of a man from another century.

"Thomas Neill Cream, also known as the Lambeth Poisoner. Poisoned 10 victims. Apprehended June 3, 1892. Hanged November 15, 1892. A rumor said his final words were a false confession that he was Jack the Ripper."

Chapter Seven

"We are not putting any credence into the ramblings of an obviously crazy, old woman. I don't care what she says, we're going to spend our day exactly as we planned. Rave will go to the bookshop, Rogue will stay here, I'll be at the gardens, and you'll take Randy to the train depot. I'll drop all of you off in town and be back to meet you at four-thirty."

"I understand and I agree. My concern is what if the kids get nervous? Maybe we should stick together just until we know they aren't afraid. I don't want to be off on a train ride when Rave needs us. We could all go to the Gardens today and then when we know everyone is all right, we'll do today's plan, tomorrow. What do you say?"

Upset, knowing her day at the Gardens alone is at risk, Rail decrees, "That's it. We're not changing our plans. If Rave gets scared, she can call one of us. I'll be happy to leave the Gardens and get her if she calls me, but you'll be a block away."

"Yeah. If we haven't left on the train. You know, the train even allows dogs on the days they give rides, they just can't go in the dining car but that's out anyway."

"All right, bring Rogue with you. If she wants to go with me, Rave can join me at the gardens. What do you say sweetie?"

"No. I'm fine, I still want to go to the bookshop. I promise I won't leave there, and I'll call you or Dad if I need anything. Can we go now?" Rave makes her feelings clear.

"Yes. Let's go." Read takes Rogue's leash to ensure he doesn't get loose again, as it is a miracle they haven't been asked to leave. Thankfully, Rogue doesn't have a vicious bone in his body, and he only wanted to play with the wily Scottie.

The family loads into the SUV and they begin their day once again. Rave gets dropped off first after a complete rehash of the rules and procedures for everything from a hangnail to a terror attack. She bravely enters the quaint shop and waves at her family through the window once she's safely inside. Rolling her eyes at her mother as she seeks the best chair for her day of reading.

Next Rogue, Random, and Read exit and confirm they have everything they need for their train day. Rail kisses all three of them and watches as they enter the old train station, now the train museum. After releasing some tension with a deep sigh she presses the ignition button, ready to begin her own flower-filled adventure.

Nothing happens.

She checks the car is in park, depresses the brake pedal, and presses the ignition again. Not a damn thing happens. Not a click. Not a flashing light. Complete silence.

"Dammit!" She checks all the settings she can see, making sure she didn't accidentally bump something that would keep it from engaging. Nothing is out of place. The damn car is broken. Anger fills her, this vacation has been anything but. She was so excited to visit the beautiful gardens alone. Now she'll likely be waiting for Triple-A for the next three hours. She pulls up her card information on her phone and places a call to the motorist assistance agency.

"Thank you for calling Triple-A, this is Allison, how may I make your day better?"

"Hi Allison, I hope you can make it better. My car won't start, I mean it's completely dead, nothing, no gauges, no lights on the dash, nothing."

"I'm sorry to hear that, I can absolutely help. Sounds like you've checked everything you can, so I'll send a mechanic out to meet you. He'll be able to tow it into the shop if he needs to, otherwise he'll fix it where you are as quickly as possible. Bear with me a moment while I upload your location and the details of what's going on. Okay, I've got you in. Looks like the nearest mechanic can be there in...oh. Um, four hours. If you need to leave the vehicle, please leave your membership card on the dash and he'll call you as soon as he arrives. Is there anything else I can help you with?"

"Nope. Thanks."

"Have a great day!"

"Yeah. Right." Rail hangs up and after a moment of self-pity she realizes it won't be a total bust if she can catch up with the guys and join them on their train ride. She quickly collects her tote, places her Triple-A member card on the dash, and locks it up. She rushes into the train museum hoping they aren't already on the train.

Read spots her and shock decorates his face like Christmas lights. He looks her over sensing something's wrong, he quickly makes his way through the people in line to board the train leaving Random to hold their spot.

"What's wrong?"

"Car wouldn't start. Triple-A is coming in four hours, so I figured I'd stay with you guys while I wait."

"Really? That's weird, I had it checked before our trip, got the oil changed, and a new battery, I can't imagine what it could be. I'm sorry you're stuck with us. Come on, they're boarding and Random's near the front of the line with Rogue."

"I'm just glad you're here, if this had happened at the Gardens, I would've been stuck there with all of you waiting on me over here."

"Ugh! Don't even say that. I'm glad I was close. This will be fun. We haven't been on a real train together in years." Read smiles, ready for the adventure the day might bring. Rail isn't quite as excited, but she smiles in return, maybe it won't be too bad.

Once they find their seats, Rail settles in and watches out the window. They're in their own little grouping with Read and Rail facing Randy and Rogue. The dog immediately curled up on the seat placing his chin on the arm rest. Randy is across from Rail, and they point out interesting elements to each other as they watch the scenery through their neighboring windows. Read excuses himself to check out the rest of the train. Even though the dining car isn't serving a meal, they're still open for guests to sit and enjoy a different view. A conductor is standing by the bar talking about the train, the line, the original company, and how it expanded across the south. Read can't help being fascinated and when the visitors are offered a chance to see the kitchen and sleeper car he joins without a thought. Eventually, he remembers he probably should've asked Rail and Randy to join him but eases his guilt by deciding the boy is probably enjoying the time with his mom and it wouldn't have been considerate to pull him away and leave her there alone, as he's certain she wouldn't have come.

While looking over the sleeper car, a large man bumps into Read but doesn't acknowledge his clumsy move. Read takes offense that the man didn't apologize, and he inspects the tall and wide stranger carefully. The man has a dull look on his face as if he's not fully aware of his surroundings. He's dressed in dirty, worn, dark clothes, Read thinks he may be homeless or of diminished capacity in some way. His anger turns to concern for the man's well-being in an instant.

"Hello. Is this your first time on the train tour?"

"Yes. I like trains," the man replies with a grin.

"Me too. I especially like old ones like this. She's a beauty, huh?"

"I suppose. But I like women better."

Read chuckles, "I hear that. I'm Read, what's your name?"

"Eddie."

"It's nice to meet you. Which car are you sitting in?"

"My bag is in the second car. I have two seats, so my bag has room."

"That's great. My family is in car two also. My wife, son, and our dog."

"I like dogs. But I like women better."

"Good one! I guess I'll see you back in car two. It was nice meeting you, Eddie."

"Yeah. Okay." Eddie lumbers off and Read can't shake the feeling he's seen Eddie before. Maybe they crossed paths earlier in the museum, or he saw him in car number two.

Read finds his way back to his family and they barely notice his return, they're so engrossed in the scenery. The train travels for an hour in one direction, stops in a small town for an hour, and then returns the same route back. Read is excited to watch the engine push the train back, versus pulling it like now. The train will drive in reverse the entire hour to return to the depot.

Back in the day, the train would swap around the engine for a return trip but on a short outing like this one it would take too much time. If the dining car was functioning, travelers could choose to stay on the train for lunch, but with the medical situation everyone will have to exit the train and eat in town. Read did a little research in preparation for their trip today and he wants to eat at the barbecue restaurant that's only a block from where the train stops.

When they pull into the depot Rogue jumps up in excitement, they gather their things and exit the train. Rogue needs a quick walk so Rail takes him into a wide alley.

When he's finished, she catches up with her family on the patio of Project Pig, an award-winning barbecue restaurant.

"Did you notice that really big guy in sort of worn-out clothes on the train?" Read asks.

"No. Sorry, my face was glued to the window, the scenery is gorgeous here. Why?"

"I saw him dad. He was dragging a big bag off the train when we got off here. He looked weird."

"That's not nice, we don't say mean things about people, right?" Rail asks.

"Sorry. I didn't mean to be disrespectful, he was just strange. He made me nervous."

"I talked to him, he seemed nice enough. Maybe a little slow, we need to be kind to people like him and look out for them. It's okay to feel uncomfortable, but we still need to be kind and helpful," Read expands on Rail's parenting.

"I can be kind and scared at the same time."

"That's good and I'm sure you don't need to be scared."

"I don't know, there was something about him that made my skin crawl, he looks kinda crazy."

"Randy! It's not nice to say things like that."

"Sorry, Mom. I just don't know how else to say it."

"It's that you called him crazy. He may be mentally ill and that's not a nice term for someone who has an illness. Please think about how you refer to people and be respectful."

"I'll try, but if someone scares me and looks like an ax murderer, it might be hard not to call them crazy."

"Okay. Let's deal with that the next time we meet an ax murderer," Read chuckles at his son's blunt remark.

"If we're finished eating, we should check out a couple shops before we have to be back on the train."

The three humans and one fuzzy beast explore the quaint village, taking turns watching Rogue and shopping. When the train whistle blows, they make their way back to the antique railway. They find their seats once again while Read looks for his new acquaintance Eddie, but doesn't spot him anywhere. The conductor reminded them to sit in the same seats, so it seems unlikely the big guy would've moved to another car. Read puzzles over his absence while they wait for the train to begin the return journey.

Chapter Eight

Rave has spent a quiet morning finishing her book. She almost cries when the hero saves the day and the planet survives. She was completely entranced by the story and didn't pay much attention to the comings and goings of other customers around her. She stretches and realizes she's hungry, so she finds an open seat in the café area. The shop has a glorified coffee bar set up in the front corner surrounded by a few tables. She takes out her sandwich and the soda her mom got from the vending machine.

Opening the second book she bought yesterday, as she takes her first bite, Rave looks around at the other people she can see. There are only two, an older woman with gray hair and a backpack who looks like she must hike everywhere she goes, and a younger woman with a ponytail. The younger woman is not as old as her mother but old enough to be married and have children. Rave can tell by her clothing alone since she can't see the woman's face. Rave turns her attention to the first line of the book and takes another bite.

When she's finished with her sandwich, Rave cleans up her trash and heads to the restroom. One stall is occupied, and she chooses the only stall not next to it. When she's finished and washing her hands the other stall door opens with a squeak. A woman steps behind her and Rave shifts to allow the woman some space to use the other sink while avoiding eye contact.

"Hey, it's you."

Startled Rave meets eyes with the woman in the mirror. Surprised, she turns to the red-haired woman and recognition fills in the details of their last meeting. Fear collects in her middle and her freshly washed palms begin to sweat.

"Janie, right?"

"You remembered! Let me see, I know, you're Rave the girl with the cool name. Funny us meeting in another restroom huh?"

"Yeah. Small world. So, do you live in town or are you visiting?"

"I stay nearby, most of the time. For some reason I've found myself in town yesterday and today. I've been hovering around this bookshop all morning. How about you?"

"I'm visiting with my family. My dad wanted to come here because of the train, it's some special historical thing. I don't know, I don't really care for trains. I'm hanging out here so I can finish reading some books I bought."

"Yeah? Are they any good?"

"I finished one and just started the second one, but yeah it was great. I love fantasy."

"I never read any, but some of the trash I've seen in this shop made my cheeks heat and my bloomers almost burst into flames," Janie says with a chuckle.

"Oh. I uh, I don't read any of those types of books. I stick with young adult fantasy, it's clean and suitable for girls my age or my mother wouldn't let me read it."

"Is your mother very strict?"

"As much as anyone, nothing over the top. Well, I should probably get back to reading before she comes to pick me up. It was nice seeing you again. Maybe next time we can try for a restaurant instead of the restroom." Rave makes an attempt at humor to ease her nerves. She can't put her finger on what's making her so nervous. Her hands are still clammy, and she feels a bit nauseous and off kilter.

Rave takes a step toward the door and Janie stops her by saying, "I'm afraid I can't let you leave Rave. You spun the wheel."

Rave chokes on air and looks at Janie once again, "What?"

"You heard me. You made a spin, now I get to kill you."

"What? What do you mean?"

"You're repeating yourself dear. I said I'm going to kill you now. You spun the Deadly-Go-Round and you landed on me, Sarah Jane Robinson. My friends call me Janie so maybe you should call me Sarah." Janie tilts her head and watches Rave with a hungry look on her face.

Backing away and toward the door, Rave puzzles over this new twist in her usually predictable life, "I don't understand. You're dead, and I'm supposed to kill you."

"Seems as if one of us wasn't told the right story then, doesn't it? Maybe whichever one of us lives, we can ask some more questions and see who was lied to. But you do have one thing straight, I'm absolutely dead. It's why I don't see how you can possibly kill me. But you, you're very much alive, for now." Janie closes the gap between them. Her face darkened and her eyes looked evil. Rave can't seem to look away from the dead woman threatening her life.

When Rave bumps into the door she moves fast, throwing it open and rushing out of the restroom. Not sure what to do or if the crazed lady is following her, she runs to the front counter looking for an employee to help her. The check out is empty and she scans the vicinity searching for anyone else. The entire store seems empty, and her pounding heart stutters with fear.

The restroom door closes with a soft woosh, she wouldn't have noticed the sound if her senses weren't on high alert. Her panic level increases tenfold, and she runs to the front door reasoning there might be someone on the street who can help and no matter what, being outside has got to be safer than being trapped in the building with a killer.

She pushes against the door with force, and it makes a loud noise when she bangs against it, but it doesn't budge. She yanks on the handle assuming it must pull instead of push. It doesn't move. She yanks with all her might, rattling the door hard, but it's locked in place. She spins looking behind her and there's no sign of Janie, yet.

With her back to the door, she pulls her phone from her pocket and dials nine-one-one. An error code rings out, alerting her the call didn't go through. Her phone has no bars of signal and only twenty-one percent of battery life left. She dials once more, the high-pitched error sound rings out again.

"No! This can't be happening. Where the hell are the employees?" She ducks down a bit and makes her way back to the counter. Throwing caution to the wind, she crouches down behind the high top of the checkout area and looks around for a phone with a cord. There's nothing. The cash register doesn't even have any electricity, it's an antique. There was an electronic scanner for payment by credit card when she was here yesterday, but it's turned off right now. There's no computer, nothing at all, and still no sign of an employee.

A book slams onto the counter above her head, and she jolts at the sharp sound, letting out a short scream from the shock.

"Where are you going? I'd like to purchase this book!" Janie yells after her as Rave takes off for the back of the store. Then Rave hears the scariest sound she's ever heard in her entire life. Janie laughs the hysterical laugh of a homicidal lunatic and it chills her blood in her veins.

Rave seeks a place to hide while still hoping there's an employee somewhere. There has to be someone here, where could they have gone? She spots an Employees Only door and tries the knob. It twists in her hand and opens to a dim back room. There's a desk in the far corner of a small office, its surface haphazardly stacked with papers and books, a computer sleeps there, and there's a phone charging cord and a stand, but no phone. Rave quickly plugs in her phone and tries the computer. It won't wake up. She checks the cord and finds it unplugged. She reconnects the computer to the electrical outlet and waits for the welcome screen to appear.

"Dammit!" she mutters when it won't let her do anything without a password. She searches the vicinity and in the drawers of the desk but doesn't find anything that might be a password. Looking closely at the room she follows the shelves which are covered in books and line three walls. There's a small table in the opposite corner of the outer room. It's like a TV tray with a tiny microwave and a box with some silverware in it. There's one somewhat sharp looking knife, at least the blade comes to a point, she holds it in her hand for security and it eases the trembling.

"Shit! What am I going to do? Think Rave, come on." A thought comes to her, and she leaves the office in search of a back exit. There's a door with a huge sign which reads, Alarm Sounds When Opened! Do NOT open! Emergency Exit Only! She quickly decides her circumstances constitute an emergency and presses the bar to open the door. Nothing. She pushes harder. Still nothing.

Realization sets in, she's trapped in this book shop alone as far as she can tell, with a psychotic dead woman who wants to kill her. Shaking her head she refuses to accept her fate implied by this predicament and runs back to the office in search of a better weapon than a small and possibly dull blade.

Finding nothing of use, she quietly leans out the door and peers around looking for red hair. Not seeing any signs of her quarry, she stays low and moves to the farthest corner of the bookshop. She hasn't investigated that section yet.

Somewhere near the front of the store she hears a loud bang, as if a book has been slammed onto a table. Like earlier, it startled her, and she almost let out a screech of fear. She continues on her journey to explore the farthest region of the shop. This section of the store is non-fiction and filled with books about How to Talk to Yourself with Kindness, and other self-help mumbo-jumbo that she'd never read in a million years. She ignores the cheesy titles and keeps her ears perked for any sign of the psycho, while still scanning for anyone who might be able to help. Finding nothing useful and nobody to save her she decides the next best option she has is to break out of the shop.

Devising a plan, she works her way silently back to the front of the store. Expecting to see the red-haired crazy lady at the checkout desk she's surprised when it's empty and a cold finger slides up her spine delivering a chill that makes her shiver. The hair on her neck stands on end and her heart pounds in her ears. She forces herself to focus on the task at hand while still listening for any sign of an impending attack.

She carefully lifts the small wooden stool from behind the counter and carries it to the window next to the door. Turning it over so it stands on the seat with the legs in the air, she hefts it up as high as she can, over her shoulder and with a twist of her body and all the strength she

can muster, she slams the chair against the plate of glass.
Holding her breath for the impending shatter of glass and
ready to bolt out of the way, she's shocked when the chair
bounces off the window and clatters to the floor. It was as
if the glass was made of elastic and the chair just bounced
right off the surface.

Disappointed but still trying to keep her wits about her,
she sighs to relieve some of the adrenaline flooding her
body. Her fight or flight reflex is struggling to break free,
since it's just as trapped as Rave, it squirms uncomfortably
beneath her skin.

Not wanting to be a sitting duck but also hoping to gain
the attention of a person on the sidewalk, she sits on the
floor with her back to the door. She retrieves the little knife
from her pocket, where she stuffed it to carry the stool. She
turns the blade over in her hand and prays it will be enough
to fight off whatever the red-haired beast is made of, she's
dead after all.

Rave ponders how a dead woman can be in this quaint
little shop and hunting her down. She thinks over what
Elvira told her. You must kill your assignment before they
kill you or you won't be able to leave. Could it be possible
that she can't leave the bookshop unless she kills Janie?
How can this be real?

With all of her fears and disbelief swirling in her mind,
she doesn't notice when Janie gets close until she drops
a book on the floor right next to Rave, who screams

and takes off running away from Janie, her crazy laughter echoing off the walls.

Panting for breath, Rave stops next to the bathroom door. She pulls it open and looks around inside. There are no windows, no weapons, she doesn't spot anything helpful at first. But then she sees another door in the mirror, she tentatively moves into the restroom to investigate. Assuming the door will be locked, she's pleasantly surprised when it opens after she turns the knob. Inside she finds cleaning supplies and a small toolbox. She quickly rifles through the tools and chooses two screwdrivers which she puts into her pockets and a hammer goes into her belt loop hanging at her side. She eyes the bottles of cleanser and chooses the biggest one and makes her way out of the restroom. She listens to the door first, then she looks out like a scared mouse venturing from its burrow with an owl watching from a nearby rooftop.

When she determines the coast is clear, she stays low and carries the cleanser with her. She needs a place to hole up and get prepared, deciding the office is a good spot, she stays close to the rear wall and keeps low enough not to be seen above the bookshelves. When she has the door barricaded, she moves things around the office making it as much of a fortress as possible. She clears off the desk and turns it, so it's between her and the door, as a secondary barrier.

She removes the lid from the cleanser and tears off a strip of her shirt, then stuffs it into the bottle leaving a tail hanging out like she's seen in the movies. She puts the hammer and one screwdriver on the desk, while keeping one screwdriver and the knife in her pockets. When she's finished, she sits in the chair to wait. This might take a while since Janie hasn't been very aggressive despite her promises to kill Rave. The red-haired murderess seems to be enjoying toying with Rave and the realization makes her skin pebble with fresh goosebumps.

Chapter Nine

Read continues to keep an eye out for his new friend, Eddie, but he doesn't spot him anywhere. When they're disembarking from the train back at the station in town, he looks at the small sea of people, knowing if Eddie was here, he'd be obvious with his extreme size reaching above the average sized people coming off the train. There's no sign of him, Read shrugs and takes Rogue's leash to lead him from the iron horse.

After using the restroom and walking Rogue, the family walks toward the book shop to collect their missing member. As they walked, Randy rehashed the train ride, excitingly relaying his favorite part of the trip was when they let him shovel a scoop of coal from the coal car and into the hot fire of the engine.

"I didn't know it could get so hot. I always thought engineers had cushy jobs, but shoveling coal into that hot oven is hard work. I'm not going to be an engineer when I grow up, I'm going to make video games. It's indoors with no shoveling."

"Sounds like you've got a plan to be lazy. Even building video games is a hard job."

His eyes go wide with shock, Randy asks for more of his dad's wisdom, "I don't want to be lazy, I just don't want to shovel coal into an oven. What other jobs do you think I could do?"

"I think you'd be great at anything on the computer and building video games, but I also think you'd make a good scientist or a teacher. You have some time before you need to decide. We could send you to a STEM camp this summer if you want, maybe you'll find something you really like while you're there."

Now his eyes spark with excitement and his grin lights up his face, "Yeah! I wanna go to a STEM camp. I heard they built robots last summer and then had a battle with them."

"Sounds like fun. We'll get you registered when we get back home. Is that the book shop?"

"Yeah. It's where I left her, but it looks empty doesn't it? I wonder if they closed early or something." Rail checks her phone for a message from Rave.

"Maybe the windows are tinted, and it just looks closed," Read offers, hoping he's right, and Rave is curled up with her book inside.

Random rushes ahead and pushes on the door, it doesn't budge. He pulls and nothing happens. He shoots a nervous look over his shoulder and tries pushing again, praying the door will magically open.

"It's locked," he reports.

Read tries the door more forcefully and it makes a loud noise but doesn't move at all. Rail cups her hands to the glass and peers into the shop. The lights are on, but she doesn't see anyone inside. Her face twists a bit when she chews on the inside of her cheek a self-soothing mechanism that isn't doing its job.

"Read, I don't see anyone in there, where would she go? Why didn't she leave me a message? Why doesn't she answer?" Her voice raises to a high-pitched panicked noise at the end of her sentence. Fear cracks her smooth façade leaving her shaky and scared for Rave.

"We need to check some of the other shops. Come on, maybe she's in one of them and something happened to her phone. You know she can't remember to charge it." Read tries to be reasonable and calm. They walk next door to the bakery.

When the door opens Read steps inside and his senses are overwhelmed by the delicious smell of baked goods. He looks around and finds the staff moving in synchronicity while scurrying behind the counter, like a squad of manic cheerleaders.

"Hi! I'm Lizzy, welcome to Hangman's Bakery. How may I help you today?" the dark haired and tattooed girl asks matter of factly.

"Thanks. Uh, we're looking for our daughter. Have you seen her?" Read holds up his phone for the girl to see a close-up photo of Rave from just a few months ago.

The waitress shuffles uncomfortably. "Sorry. I haven't seen her, but I'll keep an eye out. Can I get you folks something to drink?"

"We'll all have some water. Also, a lemon for mine, please. Thank you so much," Rail orders.

"It's my pleasure." The youngish waitress sashays through a door and into the kitchen, she returns quickly with three cups of water and a bowl.

"I thought your dog might be thirsty," she explains when Read eyes the bowl.

"Thank you so much, that was very thoughtful." Rail smiles pleasantly.

"Would you like anything else?"

Rail looks at Read then she and Lizzy wait for him to respond, but he's lost in thought and staring at his phone.

His multiple texts to Rave remain unread and there's no reply. It finally sinks in that he was asked a question.

"Oh. Uh. I'm sorry. No, we don't need anything else right this minute, thank you."

"Sure. Have a great day!" Lizzy wanders off to join the rest of the cheerleaders in what can only be described as a choreographed routine, but they're cleaning and filling orders instead of belting out cheers.

"Call her Rail, let's see if we can get through to her and find out where she is. My calls aren't going through. The older messages are unopened, and the newer ones failed to go through. There must be some interference or something here," he observes.

"She's not answering." Rail shakes her head with her phone pressed to her ear.

"Let's try a few more shops, which ones look like they have a place for her to sit and read?"

"What about that one dad?"

Randy points out a small candy shop, there's a few tables outside and it looks like they have more inside. The trio plus Rogue cross the street and look in Hanging Candy Land. Still no sign of Rave, and Rail is becoming increasingly nervous as time passes without word from their first born.

Read dials his phone trying her once again, this time it seems to connect though there's a few weird beeps and clicking sounds on the line. At least it's actually ringing this time, and he holds his breath hoping for an answer.

"Dad! Where are you? I need hel...ca oo ere ee? Hel? Dad? If oo can ear me call or hel...m tuck in boo op! Tr ng ill me!"

"We're coming! Hang on!" he shouts at the family.

"Come on! We need to get into the bookshop. She's trapped." Read takes off running back across the street and two doors down. He doesn't look back to see if Rail and Randy are following, he scans the area for something he can use to hit against the door or the window. He spots a door stop that looks to be made of steel and is a good size. When he lifts it, the weight is substantial.

"You better get back," he announces to his audience.

"I'm going to look for something to chuck at the big window, then I'm calling the police," Rail tells Read in response.

He bashes the door with the heavy metal dog, but it doesn't budge, there's not a scratch on the ancient glass. He looks at the door stop and feels the heft of the weight of it, the thing is solid, he can't discern why it won't leave a mark let alone smash it to bits. He backs up and chucks it at the large window. It bounces off like the glass is made of rubber and almost knocks his head off his shoulders. Thankfully, he has quick reflexes and ducks in time, the stone sidewalk can't dodge the falling object, and it becomes permanently scarred by the ugly but cute pug.

Rail returns with a rock filling her palm, she raises it above her shoulder poised to throw it at the window.

"Wait! Be careful, I almost got killed by a flying dog when it bounced back in my face instead of breaking the glass. Throw it so it won't hit you if it bounces off."

She turns slightly to the left and throws the rock as hard as she can, it hits the glass with a thud! Then it flies off in another direction without leaving a dent behind.

"What the heck? How is this glass so hard to break? Is it bulletproof or something?"

"Dad! I saw someone moving in the back of the store! Do you think it's Rave?" Randy calls out after seeing a dark humanoid form against the pale wall near the rear of the shop.

Both of his parents cup their eyes and lean on the glass hoping for a glimpse of their missing daughter. When Rail spots movement, she gasps.

"Oh my God! I see something! Did you see that shadow move?" she asks no one in particular.

"Oooh! I just saw something! You wait here, I'm going to the back of the building and trying the door. Don't move. Call me if she comes out." Read takes off around the corner while mother and son continue to look inside for any sign of Rave.

As they watch, Rave emerges from the rear of the shop through a door. She's staying low and looking from side to side. She doesn't look at her family then Rail bangs on the window with her palm trying to catch Rave's attention, so she'll know they're waiting outside for her. Finally, Rave spots them and she rushes forward toward her family looking relieved like a burden has been lifted from her shoulders.

As they both watch, a red-haired woman begins to chase Rave and she's holding a long weapon of some sort, maybe a stick or a pipe. Turning around, Rave holds up her hands in defense and backs away from the woman.

"No! What's happening? Baby, get away from that lady! She looks crazy, Rave!" Rogue barks and smacks his front paws against the glass as if he's trying to break it as well.

"I thought we can't call people crazy?"

"Not now Randy, we need to help your sister! Come on, grab that metal dog statue." Rail and Random begin banging the heavy dog and another rock against the glass at the same time, continuing even though it's having no effect.

Without warning as Rail watches in horror, the woman swings what they can now see is a wooden mop handle through the air aiming for Rave's head. Rogue growls a dangerous low sound they've never heard from him before.

"Look out!" Rail screams at Rave in vain. It seems her daughter can't escape and can't hear them calling to her.

Rave is quick and she moves out of the arc of the mop handle, then she stumbles a little trying to step away from the seemingly angry lunatic. The woman pounces on her, and she falls to the ground with the woman on top of her, the lady presses her stick across Rave's throat and Rail has no doubt she's trying to kill her only daughter. Instinct has her cover her son's eyes to prevent him watching his sister's murder unfold before him.

"Mom! We have to help her!"

"I'm trying!" Rail screams as she yanks on the door once again. She tugs and pulls, then kicks the door. Randy redoubled his efforts to break the glass and while they both fight to get to Rave, she fights to stay alive as her attacker works to snuff out her too short life.

Rail doesn't even notice the tears pouring down her cheeks as she screams in agony, unable to help her eldest child fight for her survival. As she watches Rave struggle beneath the weight of the red head, she can't stop trying to open the door or break the impossibly rubber glass.

Using the last of her strength, Rave uses her legs to kick at her assailant, she isn't strong enough to escape the mad woman's grasp. Her throat is being compressed, she's unable to inhale breath. As the world begins to fade with bright sparks of dying synapses, she remembers the screwdriver in her pocket and clutches it with the strength she has left. She tries desperately to speak and warn off the crazed woman, but the harbinger of death just leans harder against Rave's delicate trachea. With no other choice, Rave forces the spike of the Phillip's head screwdriver into the chest of the red-haired beast, killing her. Only now it's Rave doing the killing.

Janie collapses next to Rave, finally releasing the pressure against her neck and allowing Rave to take a desperate breath. She coughs with the pain in her almost crushed throat as the air rushes past the raw section allowing her lungs to fill and the gray swirls in her vision to fade.

Simultaneously, the door lock clicks, and Rail is able to throw open the antique barrier and rush to Rave. Tears fall from her eyes as she coughs, making it impossible for her to speak. When her mother helps lift her from beneath the attempted murderer, Rave wraps her arms around her mother and for the first time in a long time, both women are just happy to hold one another.

Chapter Ten

Read enters from the back of the shop and kicks the broom handle from the vicinity of the woman who attacked his daughter. He holds his family in an embrace and his own eyes tear up but he's able to keep his tears from falling. Rogue sniffs the feet of the corpse and makes a sound of disgust under his breath.

"I can't get anyone to answer nine-one-one. Can you get through dad?" Randy says, looking at his phone. When Read tries, he gets the angry beeps of a failed call.

"How can nine-one-one be out of service?" Rail asks.

Rave waves her hands and finally gains the attention of her family. She can't speak, every attempt causes a coughing outbreak, and she holds her throat trying to tell them she can't talk.

"Okay, you can't talk but you want to tell us something. Go ahead, do your best."

Rave nods slightly and tries to explain in a low whisper without hurting her injured vocal cords, "It was the Deadly-Go-Round, Janie was my spin." Rogue licks her cheek and wags his tail.

"But that's not possible. It's just a silly table, it's not really cursed or whatever, I mean..." Rail looks at Janie's dead body sprawled and bleeding on the floor, a screwdriver protruding from the center of her chest, her face frozen in a mask of death, her eyes vacant. Rail's own eyes are wide, and she shivers as the circumstances sink in. It wasn't until Rave killed Janie that they were able to get into the shop, the lock just clicked open at that exact moment.

"Read? How did you get into the back of the building?"

"I was trying everything to get the door open, I was smashing it, kicking it, yanking on it, and suddenly the lock clicked, and it opened like nothing. I ran inside and found you all here with Rave and the maniac. Why?"

"I think Rave's right. You saw how hard we tried to get into the building, but the moment she killed Janie, the lock immediately disengaged, and the door opened. Remember what Elvira said, you can't leave until you make the kill. What if she wasn't just trying to scare us? What if it's true and we have to make a kill to get out of here?"

"Let's get our stuff and leave. If something stops us, then we'll worry about what the truth might be. Come on, let's get out of here. Maybe we can call the police from the inn."

They gather themselves and exit the shop. Rogue bravely leads the way as the family follows, but when they reached the spot where Rail left the car, it's gone. There are large tire marks in squiggly lines where the SUV used to be parked. Looking at the marks, Rail dials her phone.

"Triple A, how may I help you?" A chipper voice blares from her phone's speaker.

"Hi, this is Rail Ripley, I had some car trouble, and you said it would be four hours before the tow truck could come. I didn't leave the keys, but the vehicle is gone. Where did you tow it?"

After giving the operator her membership information, she hears a response she wasn't prepared for, "I'm sorry Mrs. Ripley, when the driver got to where you said you left the vehicle, it wasn't there. We didn't tow it anywhere. Is there anything else I can help you with today?"

"You haven't helped me at all. Where the heck is my car?"

"I can't say ma'am, but I know for a fact we didn't touch it. The driver reported it wasn't there. Well, if there's nothing else I can do for you, have a great day!"

"Wait! We need help, we can't get through to nine-one-one, can you please send the police to where you sent the tow driver?"

"Maybe you should've listened to Elvira. Have a great day!" Click! Rail jolts at the loud noise of disconnection.

"What the heck was that? What the heck is happening?"

"You can say the curse words mom, I've heard them before. Mikey Stratton says all of them at school, he even got detention when Mr. Mills heard him say the 'A' word."

Read asks, "What's the 'A' word?"

"Ass," Randy whispers like he's in church.

"Aaah, thanks son, but I think your mother is in the habit of substituting curse words. But if things go much worse, I may pull out a few. Let's say we all have a free pass for curse words until we get through whatever's happening."

"Deal." Random fist bumps his dad.

"How can you be so calm? Our daughter almost died, and she had to kill a person to save herself. We have no car to escape, and we can't get hold of anyone to help us. It's crazy and it can't be real, but it is. I think I'm going to need all the curse words!"

"I'm just trying to be calm for the kids. You're right it's bizarre. We need to see if we can find someone who can help us and a way to call the police. Come on, let's try the bakery with that weird bouncy girl, maybe they have a phone that works."

Rail supports Rave as they walk to the bakery, she's okay but it makes Rail feel better. Rave has completely accepted the reality of their dire situation, unlike her parents who still think there must be a logical explanation that doesn't involve a spinning table.

When they reach the bakery, the door is locked, and the lights are off. No cheerleaders move in synchronicity inside. The family looks up and down the street for anyone who may be able to help them and find the place deserted. Randy is feeling his nerves twist uncomfortably in his stomach despite his father's efforts to keep the mood positive. Rogue is on high alert, his ears are perked, and his hair stands up, especially on his back and neck. Rave wonders if it's like when people get a chill on the back of their necks.

"Okay. What do we do now?" Rail asks.

"Let's try the train station, it was bustling when we left. Maybe someone is still around or we can use a phone."

As they approach the door, Read has hope, he can see the lights are on. The door opens when he tugs on it and the family enters the old building. Rail leads Rave to a bench and has her sit with Randy and Rogue, then she and Read check for anyone who might be able to help while searching for a phone. Read checks the shop while Rail checks the ticket counter and office. Finding no one and no phones, not even inside the office, they sit on a bench across from the kids to think.

"You should stay here, at least it's inside. I'm going to check the train and the other buildings and see if I can find anyone around. If not, we may have to walk back to the inn. It's only a couple miles so I think we can make it. Rave, do you still have snacks?"

"I don't have my bag. I left it in the book shop. I have my phone in my pocket, nothing else," she whispers and then breaks into a coughing fit.

"Okay, why don't you try looking for something to eat." he mostly states to his wife. "But don't get out of sight of the kids, while I check outside. I'll be back in ten minutes or less. Don't leave this building no matter what." Read stands and Rail jumps to her feet, hugging him and wiping tears from her eyes. Rave and Randy hug him, and he pats Rogue before leaving through the back door.

Rail begins her search by trying the barred door of the ticket booth. When it opens, she carefully looks around making sure no one is inside. Then she checks every drawer in search of anything that might help them. Most of the drawers are empty. The top drawer contains some pens, paperclips, stickers, and a letter opener which she sets on top of the counter. It's the first item in her pile of helpful things.

Outside, Read checks the other doors to the building he just left and finds them all locked. He moves to a smaller building and tries the doors there with the same result. He moves to the train platform, finding no people or items to help them, he climbs the steps to the train. Once on board he searches methodically for anything useful in their current situation.

He finds a granola bar still in the wrapper pushed into the corner of a seat. A hat is on the floor underneath another old-style train bench. When he enters the dining car, he feels like he's hit the jackpot when he discovers a tray filled with silverware including a few sharp steak knives. He puts them in his pocket and makes a mental note not to sit with them in his pocket.

Next, he finds some bottles of water and packets of crackers. He searches for something to carry them in and when he doesn't find anything, he makes a satchel out of a tablecloth. Stacking the items in the middle and pulling the corners into his hand to hold the items. He checks the kitchen area and finds the refrigerator completely empty, wiped clean and standing open. He recalls the illness tainting the local food serving establishments and turns to the dry goods in the pantry. He finds huge containers of flour, sugar, and dry pasta. There are canned vegetables and tomato sauce, ketchup and mustard in bottles, and a wall of spices and seasonings. The only food he sees a use for are some vanilla wafer cookies. Everything else is just an ingredient that requires fresh items to become anything. He puts the box of wafers into his sack, feeling like Santa, he gets it over his shoulder and makes his way to the rest of the cars.

When he reaches car number two, he's startled to find a person in one of the seats. He stops in his tracks and assessing the scene before him he decides to set his sack of food on a seat close to him. Then it dawns on him that he recognizes the person sitting in the window seat with their head leaned against the window frame.

He approaches and when he can see their face, he sees their eyes are closed and there's a large bag on the seat next to them. While he debates if he should wake the sleeping giant, the man's eyes pop open and Read jolts at the movement.

"Oh! Hey, Eddie, you scared me. I'm glad to see you here, do you have a phone by any chance?"

"No. Don't have one."

"Okay. Are you alright?"

"Yes."

"My family and I are stranded here, our car was towed, and we haven't been able to get through to the police, or anyone to help us. Actually, you're the first person we've seen, since, uh, since we figured out, we're stuck. Did you see anyone on the train when you came on board?"

"No."

"Okay. Um, I need to get back inside to my family. Do you wanna come with me? You can stay with us until we find help if you want. Unless you have a car?"

"No car."

"So, do you want to come with me?"

"Okay."

The big man stands and maneuvers out of the seat and collects his bag which is quite bulky and looks heavy. The large man makes it seem lighter than it must be. He steps out from between the seats and motions for Read to lead the way. After collecting his own bulky bag, he follows the aisle to the exit from the train and carefully navigates the steps to the ground.

"So, Eddie, what do you do for a living?"

"They call me a butcher. How about you?"

"I work with computers, nothing exciting."

"I enjoy my work."

"I wish I could say the same. I always wanted to be a rock star. I think I would've enjoyed making music, but computers pay the bills."

"Where is your family?"

"They're just inside the depot."

"Then I better do this now." Read turns around to see what his friend is talking about and he sees something coming at him from the corner of his eye, he tries to duck but with a sharp thwack! His head feels like it's imploding, and bright lights explode in front of his eyes, he thinks to himself, this must be what they mean by 'seeing stars' because I see them.

"What happened?" Read questions as he spots Eddie bringing a crowbar down toward him again. He rolls onto his side and the bar stabs into the ground right where his head was, only a moment ago.

It suddenly dawns on him that his friend, Eddie, is trying to kill him. He unsuccessfully tries to lift himself from the dirt while his attacker wrestles the curved metal bar from the ground. Raising it once again, Eddie aims for Read's torso this time and Read rolls once more, but the bar catches his left shoulder sending shooting pain down his arm and into his head reigniting the excruciating pain behind his eyes. The pressure is so strong his eyes water, further blurring his vision.

"Why... are you...doing...this?" Read fights to get the words out while he works to stand.

Eddie stops and appears thoughtful, "I have to kill you. It's what happens when you spin the Go-Round, it's not fun and I can't even keep your head, but I have to kill you because they hurt me if I don't. I only like to make things with skin and bones, it's wasteful to bury the bodies, if I don't make things, Mother will be mad."

Confused but understanding exactly what's happening at the same time, Read is unsteady on his feet and his head and shoulder throb in time with his heartbeat. He reaches into his pocket and retrieves the knives, needing only one, he drops the others.

"What's your full name, Eddie?"

"I'm The Butcher of Plainfield."

"I meant what's your legal name?"

"Edward Gein."

"How did you get here? Did you walk? Or drive?"

"No. I'm always here. If the Go-Round lands on me, I have to kill who they say. They don't let me kill unless it lands on me. It's no fun."

"Who are they?"

"They're mean. I don't like them, they lie. They always say if I kill, they'll set me free, but they never do, but I still have to do what they say. Are you my friend?"

"I thought I was, but you're trying to kill me so I'm going to have to say no."

"Okay." Ed swings the crowbar at Read's head. Anticipating the strike he's able to avoid being hit and since Ed committed hard to the move, Read's able to stab him with the steak knife right between the ribs. Eddie drops the crowbar and looks at Read, his face sad. His arms fall to his sides and on his next inhale he coughs, sending blood splatter across his lips.

Read steps back, holding the bloody blade out in case he has further use for it. His would-be killer begins to waiver, his knees buckle, and he falls to the ground on top of his crowbar. He continues to watch Read, who watches him right back, neither man needing to voice their regrets.

When the light has completely left his foe, Read sits on the ground and shudders. He counts his blessings and thinks about each member of his family and how much he loves them even though they're each capable of being incredibly difficult. When he considers his frustrating daughter, he remembers she had to kill her spin. He just had to kill his, that means Random, Rail, and even Rogue have yet to complete their assignments. They could be killed in the fight, Random is just a little boy, Rail is a prissy and delicate woman never interested in sports or physical activity of any kind beyond digging in the garden. Poor Rogue, he's just a dog, a sweet friendly dog. How will he survive a battle with a serial killer?

"Oh God! Rogue's accidental spin landed on Ted-Freaking-Bundy! Shit!" Read exclaims as he picks himself up and charges for the station to find his family and protect them from what's sure to come.

Chapter Eleven

"Dad! Are you alright? What happened?" Randy questions seeing his dad's disheveled and slightly bloody appearance.

Rave, Rogue, and Rail turn to see what Randy's talking about. Rail gasps at her spouse's form, his clothing is rumpled, his temple is dripping blood, and his knees and forearms are dirty. Read approaches them and trying his best to remain calm, explains what happened to him outside.

"You're sure he's dead?" Rave looks around as if the man might come lunging at them from the shadows, her eyes are wide and scared.

"Yeah. He's definitely dead. Have you seen anyone in here?"

"No. I found a few makeshift weapons but nothing to rescue us," Rail reports.

"Oh shit! I forgot the weapons and my bag of supplies outside. We should stay together and get them. There are a few steak knives and the crowbar he used should be there as well. Come on, let's go quickly and grab that stuff."

The family walks together with Rogue in the lead, his nose to the ground. When they get outside, Read leads them with Rogue to the spot where he left everything. He stops in his tracks when he sees the dead man is not where he left him. Randy walks into the back of Read and they all stop. Looking where Read is staring with a shocked look on his face, they can see a tablecloth filled with items from the train and a crowbar nearby. When they step closer, Rave spots some steak knives.

"Dad? Are you okay? Here are the knives." She points down while keeping her eyes trained on her father. His face is pale, his jaw slack, his eyes frozen in terror.

Rail steps to her husband's side and gently touches his arm. Even though she did her best not to startle him, he jumps at her touch.

"What is it?" she asks.

"He was right here. He was lying on top of the crow-bar. I know he was dead, his eyes went blank, he stopped breathing, there was blood pouring out of his chest. Where's the blood? Where's the dead body?" He steps forward and examines the ground more closely and sees the steak knife that was next to the body where he dropped it. The other knives are still scattered by the sack of sup-plies. He looks around, spinning, searching desperately for something.

"What is it, Dad?"

"His bag. He had a huge bag with him, but I don't see it either. I wasn't inside more than a few minutes ago. How could someone move his body, move his bag, and clean up all of the blood from the grass so quickly? How would you even clean blood from grass?" he asks in astonishment.

"I told you, it's true. It's supernatural," Rave whispers, holding her sore throat.

"I believe her, Rave had to fight that lady, she would know," Randy offers his opinion.

"Maybe we should stow the supplies and go back to the book shop and see if that body's gone too."

"Yeah. But I'm bringing the supplies. Apparently if you take your eyes off something around here, it vanishes."

Read gives Rave and Rail a knife and keeps one for himself, tucked into his pocket. Random lifts the crowbar and rests its heavy metal weight on his shoulder like a baseball bat. The group stays close together and watches for movement as they make their way to the bookshop.

When they arrive in front of the door, Rave can already see the body is gone. The blood is gone too, but everything else is exactly how they left it.

Rave looks around the shop and when an idea comes to her, she says, "Why don't we barricade the doors after we double check nobody's here? Then we can make a safe place to stay where we can keep an eye on the street and watch for any sign of people who might be able to help us."

Looking around and assessing the big windows and comfortable sofas, he agrees it's a good place to hole up and wait for help or until they come up with a better plan. Nodding, he takes Rogue around to check if anyone else is in the building. They search in the back office and the omnisex restroom, finding no one alive or dead, he agrees to set up a stronghold in the shop.

"Do you have your phone charger?" Rail asks Rave.

"If my bag is still here, I will."

"I'll go with you to find it."

They return moments later with Rave's bag and all the items she left inside are still there. She plugs in the phone cord and attaches her phone. A satisfying green light with a bolt of lightning illuminates the top corner of her screen. However, no bars appear next to it reminding her there's no service. A frown tugs at her mouth.

"Let's organize our supplies and see what we have. We can stack them on the service counter," Rail suggests proactively.

After a few minutes they have a pile of snacks, bottled water, a granola bar, some pouches of cookies and chips, and two sandwiches from the kitchen at the inn. The weapons are laid out, so they'll be easy to grab. In addition to the weapons Read gathered from the train, they collect Rave's hammer, screwdrivers, knife, and the Molotov cocktail of cleanser. Rail added her letter opener to the weapons area and the bag of donuts she found in the employee break room at the train station goes into the food pile.

Now that they have everything organized, they aren't sure what to do with themselves while they wait. Are they waiting for help or to be killed? That thought is what they want to avoid.

Random has an idea, "I'm going to get something to read." He hops up and aims for the science aisle, checking the signs on the end of the shelf he finds it quickly. When he stops at the robotics section, his mom passes him and looks over the gardening books. Rail notices a Local section and abandons her flowers for a more practical topic. She perused the books there reading the titles on the spines.

History of Hangman's Bluff, and A Guide to Hangman's Antiques, capture her attention. She pulls both titles and heads to a table. She glances through the History book first and finds a chapter about the inn where they're staying, where they came into contact with that evil table.

When she turns onto page thirteen, her mouth falls open. There on the page is a photo of the disturbing table. The heading reads, Deadly-Go-Round. She skims the paragraphs below and finds a disturbing bit of information.

"Ahh!" She jumps and yelps when Read touches her shoulder.

"Sorry. I didn't mean to scare you. Did you find something?"

"Yeah. Listen to this...The Deadly-Go-Round is an antique table from an unknown provenance. Very little is known about this item and it's a conversation starter at the inn where rumor has it, the table is cursed. The rumor goes on to say it was originally created by the first owner of the Hangman's Inn. It's said anyone who spins the table will become trapped in town until they dispatch the person matched to the arrow on the table at the end of their spin.

After examining the table, it was discovered to have the initials "H.H.H." and the numbers 1892, presumed to be a date. The table is made of wood local to Illinois and it's been suggested the initials belong to H.H. Holmes, and the wood was part of his home in Chicago, which was named "The Murder Castle," after his arrest and confession to more than one-hundred murders, which some experts say is likely half the actual number of deaths caused by Dr. Holmes, whose birth name was Herman Mudgett."

"Oh my God! Random spun H.H. Holmes, it didn't say very much. But there's enough to make him terrifying. Does it say anything else?"

"No. But this book might say something. Um, let's see, page thirteen, here. It's the same picture as the first book. Hmmm...it says the same thing as the first book. Oh, but there's more.

The Deadly-Go-Round was so named by the grand-daughter of the original owner of the inn. Mr. Mudgett bought the original building, which was a farmhouse, although the family who owned it prior to his purchase suddenly left the area and were not heard from again. He added on two wings leaving the original house as the lobby, parlor, kitchen, and dining room for the inn. The wings housed the added guest rooms and have two stories, the original renovation consisted of twelve guest rooms and four additional restrooms. This was added to by subsequent owners over the next century and beyond.

The historic inn is filled with a variety of antiques but none so interesting as this cursed table. The owner after Mr. Mudgett, Belle Gunness, was said to have used the inn to entice men into her trap so she could kill them. She was presumed dead in the fire that burned down the West wing of the inn in 1908. However, her demise is unconfirmed.

The table survived the fire and has been in the kitchen since the renovation after the fire in 1908. The current owner, in 2021, has items found in the safe that she claims describe the origin of the table and the consequences of spinning it. She is presently unwilling to provide those items for this author. With advice from the owner and a modicum of self-preservation, I have chosen not to spin the Deadly-Go-Round just in case there's any truth to the tales."

"Holy shit! Sorry," Read exclaims.

"It's fine, remember, we have a free pass on curse words. Nothing else covers this situation as well, I'm with you, holy shit!"

"I wish it would tell us what to do if we already spun the table."

"I think we need to go to the inn. It seems like that's where the answers will be," Rail reasons.

"Yeah, you're probably right, but it's going to be dark soon. I think we should stay here until morning and then get an early start. It's too dangerous to be exposed in the dark with murderers hunting us down."

"You're right. Let's see if we can put some of the furniture together so we can all sleep in one spot. We can take turns keeping watch and sleeping."

"I'll figure out what makes sense to move and where to put it, then we'll all work together to move everything."

"Okay. I'm going to check in with the kids and let them know the plan. Meet you back here in five." They kiss and separate to complete their tasks.

It seems the grave situation has brought out the best in Rail and Read noticed appreciating her affection regardless of the cause. She explains the plan to Rave and Randy while he assesses the available furniture and the safest location for it. Rave was right, the office area seems like a good place to sleep, with only one door to worry about, they can rest while just one of them keeps watch. If he positions a chair in the doorway of the office, they'll be able to watch the street as well.

The family works together as a team to set up their beds and Rail offers to take the first watch. Read's head is still throbbing from his fight with Eddie, so she instructs him to rest and close his eyes. She starts off her shift pacing and rehashing everything that's happening. She comes to the same conclusion as earlier the answers must be at the inn. Rail checks the front of the store often, not just keeping watch for murderers, but also hoping a savior will appear and help them get out of town.

As the clock ticks into the wee hours of the next morning her eyes become heavy and she struggles to stay alert. Thankfully Read was able to sleep and he relieves her just as she fades almost falling asleep. She has no trouble going to sleep once she's snuggled in with the kids and Rogue.

It's not until the sun glows in the windows that she wakes and feels rested enough to make the walk back to the inn.

"Good morning. Did you sleep okay?"

"Yeah, I was out. How's your head?"

"Much better. Getting a few hours of sleep last night really helped."

"Did you see anyone?"

"Nobody. Are the kids up?"

"They're awake, working on getting up. I asked them to hurry, poor Rogue needs to go out and we all have to go together."

"Let's leave everything here except the weapons. I don't think we need to drag a bunch of heavy supplies a few miles when the inn has food and water."

"Good point."

"What's a good point?" Randy asks as he enters with Rogue on his leash.

"We're not going to bring the supplies back to the inn. Where's your sister?"

"She's in the bathroom, she said she'll be right out."

Once they're all together they remove the barricade from the front door and Rogue rushes to the nearest tree and lifts his leg. The fluffy guy looks relieved, literally. As they make their way in the direction of the inn, Read keeps his head on swivel watching for killers hiding in the bushes. Rail is tense and jumpy. Rave is quiet, seemingly subdued from the events yesterday. Rail and Read both quietly worry about the trauma and long-lasting effects of her assignment.

Rogue keeps his ears perked and his nose to the ground as they walk at a steady pace. When they reach the end of the block they turn left, aiming the correct direction to get back to the inn. As they move down the block, Rail is first to notice something up ahead.

"Do you see that?"

"What?" Read asks, looking in the direction she points.

"That shop, the blue building at the end of this block, I see lights and I swear I saw movement in the window."

Read removes the knife from his pocket and holds it close to his hip. He slows his pace watching the shop in question. He catches a movement through the glass, and he takes off running while holding his hand out signaling his family to wait. They stop and watch him with bated breath.

Read slows when he gets to the corner of the building, he presses close to the building and leans over to peer inside. He doesn't move or signal for far too long and Rogue pulls against his leash wanting to join the master of the family. Rail slowly inches forward, her palm on Randy's chest keeping him behind her. Finally, Read signals for them to join him against the building.

"What's going on in there?" Rail whispers.

"People are having breakfast. There's a waitress and two guys eating at different tables. They look perfectly normal.

We should go in but keep our weapons handy. If any of them come after us, stab first and ask questions later. Rave, are you going to be alright?"

"I'm good, let's go."

She has a steak knife in her palm pointed at the ground. Read leads the way to the door, and nobody seems particularly interested in their approach. He pulls the door open and ushers his family inside. A bell chimes as the door moves.

"Sit anywhere you like, folks," the blonde waitress calls out without even looking up at them. Rail waits outside with Rogue. She watches through the window perched to join the fight if anyone attacks her loved ones.

"Actually, I think we'll make a to-go order, if that's okay?"

"Sure thing, hun. There's a menu on the counter, look it over and I'll be right with you."

Read looks at the menu but doesn't really see it. He's busy watching the other guests for any sign of impending attack, but they're focused on their breakfasts. The one man at the counter is watching the waitress's behind while he takes a bite of eggs. The other man is older and seated in a booth. He's reading a newspaper and seems completely oblivious to the family nervously waiting for service.

Read relaxes a little, it feels normal here, nothing feels off the way it did just yesterday. He focuses on the menu now, seeing some items he wants to order. He shares the menu with the kids so they can choose when the waitress comes over.

"Hi Sweetie, what can I get for ya?" The woman is at least ten years older than Read, her skin is splotchy and wrinkled. She has the look of someone who's had a hard life, and he feels something for her that's not quite pity.

"It's to-go, I'll have two breakfast burritos and two coffees. Kids, what would you like?"

Randy speaks first, "I want a sausage, egg, and cheese English muffin. And...orange juice, please."

"I'll take a cup of oatmeal and a small hot chocolate, please," Rave whispers softly.

"You got it hun. It'll be about fifteen minutes. Do you wanna have a seat while you wait?"

"Oh. Uh, we have a dog. We're gonna wait outside if that's okay?"

"Yeah, sure. I'll let you know when it's ready. Do you want a sausage patty for your pup?"

"Yeah, that'd be great. Thanks."

Read guides the kids out the door ahead of him and they meet Rail seated on a bench. Randy sits next to his mom and hugs her. She hugs him back with tears in her eyes, hoping they'll stay this connected forever.

Rave sits quietly on Rail's other side. Her throat still aches from the attack yesterday and when she was in the restroom, she could see a bruise across her neck. Her hand keeps rubbing her neck in hopes of somehow soothing her throat.

The family isn't completely at ease but the normal atmosphere they found inside the café is helping them relax enough to feel better. Randy smiles when he sees a big four by four truck turn onto the same road as the café.

"Dad, can we ask them for a ride?"

"No. I don't think we should go that far, but I'm going to ask about a phone in the restaurant. Did you see anyone else while we were inside?"

Rail responds, "No movement, not even a bird the entire time you were in there."

When the waitress waves at him, Read heads inside to collect their order. After he pays and leaves a generous tip making the waitress smile, he asks to use their phone. She puts an ancient looking phone on the counter for him.

Read glances at his family through the doors of the café and they look subdued and safe. He dials nine-one-one and can hardly believe it when it begins to ring.

"Emergency services, what's your emergency?" A bored voice answers his call.

"Yes. Hello. My family and I are stuck, um, stranded in Hangman's Bluff. My daughter was attacked in the book shop, we need the police."

"Do you need an ambulance?"

"No. Just police. Please hurry."

"What's your name?"

"Read Ripley."

"Phone number?"

"My phone isn't working, I'm at a café."

"I see that sir I still need your personal phone number."

He gives his number and then urges, "Please, send the police right away."

"I heard you the first time, sir. They've been dispatched, but I still need some information."

"Do you know the address of the incident?"

"No. But it's the book shop in town, on the main road. It's across from the train station."

"Is your daughter injured?"

"Yes. Her throat is injured, and she has some bruises and cuts. She was attacked by a crazy woman inside the book shop."

"Will you meet the officers at the book shop?"

"No. We're at Deadman's Café, around the corner, we'll wait here."

"Do you know the attacker?"

"No. I mean, we know her name, but we never met her before. She attacked our daughter unprovoked."

"Come now, Mr. Ripley, she spun the Dead-ly-Go-Round, didn't she?"

The color drains from his face and his stomach clenched unpleasantly. His eyes grow wide with shock, and he pulls the handset from his face to look at it with terror.

"How...how do you know that?"

"Everyone knows. Didn't she in fact kill Janie? And didn't you kill Eddie?"

He dropped the phone and shaking his head, he backed away from the offensive device. Not remembering how it got there, he clutches the bag holding their breakfasts and without a glance at anyone in the café fearful of what he'll see, he throws open the doors and rushes to his family.

"Run! Run! We have to get out of here! Come on!"

Rave is the first to move, she takes off in the direction they were heading before this stop. Rogue pulls against his leash, urging Rail to join Rave. She takes Random's hand and pulls him up with her. She holds out the leash to Read, who slows just enough to grab it before following Rave. Rail helps Randy get going and then they run after the others together. None of them hesitate to run as fast as possible away from the creepy, haunted town.

"What happened in there?" Rail calls.

"I got through on their phone, to the police. They aren't going to help us."

"Why not?"

"They're part of whatever is happening. Run faster!"

"Are they coming?"

"The operator said they were, but then he said it was our fault because of that damn table!"

"Oh shit!" Random exclaimed.

"I just want to get out of the town. Maybe if we can get back to the inn, we can get answers or help."

Chapter Twelve

When the blue roof of the beautiful bed and breakfast becomes visible in the distance, Rail relaxes feeling safer and closer to help. When the family climbs the stairs to the large front porch, Read stops them before they open the door to the lobby.

"We need to stay together. We don't know if this is a good idea or not. Keep your eyes open and your weapons ready," Read advises them.

Rave carefully opens the front door and looks around inside the foyer area of the lobby. When she decides the coast is clear she signals them to follow her. She stays close to the wall and leans around the threshold of the front parlor, once again checking if it's safe to advance.

The family stays close with Read at the rear, Rave and Rogue in the lead, and Rail and Randy in the middle. Rail now holds Rogue's leash, and he walks ahead of her keeping pace with Rave. They make it to the front desk without incident. Rave taps the bell resting on the countertop and watches for anyone approaching. Eventually, the man they can't remember joins them.

"Good morning, folks. How can I help you?"

"Our car was towed from town, where would they take it?" Read questions.

"I don't know sir. It depends who towed it and why."

"What's the deal with that stupid table in your kitchen?" Rail questions angrily.

"Oh, the Deadly-Go-Round? It's a fascinating antique don't you think? You folks spun it didn't you? Isn't it self-explanatory? You spin, then you must dispatch whoever it lands on, or you can't leave. Is that why your car was towed? Because that probably means it's in the police impound lot. Did you check with the police department?"

"What's wrong with you? Don't you see how crazy this is? A table that traps you unless you kill someone. Who keeps a murder table? Why does everyone just act like it's normal?" Rail demands her last visage of control snapping.

"The table has always been here, ma'am. If you don't want to participate, all you have to do is not spin it. Didn't Elvira warn you what happens if you spin it?"

Random speaks up, "She made it sound like it was just a story. She didn't tell us it was real!"

"That's unfortunate, Elvira does love her stories. Is there anything else I can help you with?"

"You haven't helped at all," Rave observes in a horse whisper.

"Would you like to speak to the manager?" the forgotten man asks.

"Yes. Call the manager."

"Please wait here, I'll make the call." The man wanders off beyond the archway to destinations unknown. They've already lost the ability to picture his face or recall anything else about him.

Rail turns to her family with her eyes tearing up, and Read steps to her side wrapping his arm around her shoulders. He holds out his other arm to Rave, including her in the embrace. Not one to require an invitation, Randy puts his arms around his mother's waist, and she pulls him closer. The family affection bolsters their spirits and infuses Read with renewed confidence that he will get his family out of this messed up town.

"Maybe waiting here for the manager isn't our best idea," Random says.

"You may be right. Let's go to our rooms and pack up our things. We can shower and change, collect some more weapons, and decide our next move." They nod in agreement and climb the stairs to the kids room first.

"Pile up only your most important items on the bed. We'll pack your backpacks and then go to our room," Read directs.

Rail helps both kids locate their electronics and charging cords. They only grab one change of clothes not wanting their packs to be too heavy. It only takes a few minutes, and they go to Read and Rail's room next. Rogue perches on his doggy bed supervising the organized chaos. Rave takes a shower first and Read pushes a dresser in front of the door for extra safety.

Randy showers next and Rave helps her mother search through their collective belongings for weapons. Rail's gardening supplies yield a pair of snips, a small shovel, and a hand rake sporting sharp claw tips. Her make-up bag offers full size and manicure scissors. They also score a pocketknife and a telescoping baton in Read's gear. He also had two flashlights and a headlamp. Rave adds a roll of duct tape to the pile.

"Where did that come from?" Rail asks.

"I forgot I had that. Remember that time the airline destroyed my suitcase when I had business in Quebec? I bought it for fifty dollars and used it to get my suitcase home. For that price I kept it just in case I needed it again.

Luckily, I had it because when we went to the Bahamas, it's how I repaired your broken heel."

"I forgot about that. I almost broke my ankle, but your fix held all night."

"Duct tape has many uses." Read smiles remembering the trip was when he and Rail were much happier. With a tilt of his head he scrutinized his still beautiful wife and determined to make more of an effort with her.

Still packing items in backpacks and her tote, Rail waves Read ahead of her for the shower. He takes his clean outfit and hurries into the bathroom.

Rogue drinks water but refuses to eat, he's as much on edge as his family. He keeps his ears perked, listening for danger and prepared to protect his humans.

When Read steps out of the bathroom shrouded in a cloud of steam, Rail kisses his cheek on her way past as she takes her turn in the shower. When she removes her rumpled, dirty clothes it feels better. She brushes out her hair and scrubs her teeth of two-day old plaque. When she turns on the water in the shower, she hears a strange noise and turns it off again listening.

Right as she starts the hot water, she hears it again. It's a muffled clanging sound or banging. Ignoring it as an old pipe, she steps into the shower. When she leans her head back to scrub the shampoo into her scalp, she notices a hatch in the ceiling. She assumed that there must be access for the attic above.

As she watches, the hatch moves a little as if something or someone above is trying to open the horizontal door. She hurries through her shower, rushing the scrubbing and conditioning, while never taking her attention away from that opening. When she's as clean as possible for such fast washing, she wraps her hair in a towel and rapidly dries her body with another. Her eyes continue to examine the hatch. She can hear the movement above.

Then a loud bang startles her, and she runs for the door to escape. It won't open, she twists the lock this way and that, turning the knob and yanking on the door, it's stuck closed. She yells for her family, but they don't respond. She can hear the TV through the door and conversation between everyone, but somehow, they can't hear her.

When something clatters loudly against the opening and the hatch springs open an inch, she presses her back to the door and watches it carefully. When it silently opens two inches she jolts forward and wrangles her clean clothes, wrestling her damp body into the fabric sticking to her skin. When she's in her clothes, twisted as they may be, she stands just out of the way of the hatch watching, and listening intently.

When it's quiet for a moment, she tries the door again, banging on it and yelling as loud as she can. Still, her family doesn't respond and she's unable to muscle the door open. Giving up, she checks out the small window above the toilet and decides there's no way she could fit through the tiny opening, even if she could get it open. Which she wasn't able to do when she tried. Frustrated, she looks at the hatch to the attic and wonders if there's a way out up there and what else is up there.

Without warning there's a loud bang and the door in the ceiling falls open, extending a ladder to the ground at her feet causing her to jump and release a small squeal. She looks up into the pitch-black hole in the ceiling and shivers at the thought of going up there, in the dark. But she realizes quickly she's trapped and if she has to enter the attic to complete her assignment, so be it. She clutches the knife that was still in her discarded pants and climbs slowly up the ladder.

She's never been so brave, but the events in this crazy town have shifted something inside her, and whether it's a nightmare and she'll wake from safely in her bed, or if it's reality, she's come to the conclusion she must continue on. When her head breaches the opening into the room above, she twists from side to side trying to see if anyone is perched to attack. Seeing nothing of note, she carefully pulls herself up onto the wooden floor and sits with her feet still on the top step of the ladder allowing her eyes to adjust to the dim light only alleviated by the light shining up from the bathroom below.

She hears a sound to her right and spins in that direction. Squinting her eyes she tries to peer into the dark and discern the reason for the noise. It sounds like a heavy chain being dragged across a wood floor. Out of the corner of her eye she sees something disappear, it could be a mouse or maybe it was a chain. Curiosity takes her closer, she stands and reaches out her hands feeling for anything that might bump her head. Her feet shuffle as she attempts to avoid anything on the floor waiting to trip her.

As she slowly moves across the room, she can tell there's a glow coming from around a corner. It's a soft glow as if from a candle. She peeks around the corner and indeed finds a candle on a table projecting long shadows from the items close to it. A dress form for a seamstress creates a headless shadow and a coat rack makes a large, long-necked monster shadow flicker on the ceiling.

She can't see what's beyond the bright flame of the candle, it makes purple flames dance in front of her eyes causing the dark to be even more impossible to penetrate. She concludes there must be another exit from the attic if a candle has been left burning here. Someone had to have left the candle. As she passes the candle the darkness beyond begins to come into focus and she spies some more pieces of furniture and useless junk.

A movement in the far corner catches her eye and she freezes in place waiting for her eyes to readjust and the cause of the commotion to be revealed. As the dark begins to fade into a dim gray illumination, she sees large loops upon the wall with thick chains running through them. As she watches, the chains slide inside their circles and a dark figure stands in the corner, rising from the floor to his full height.

She can't see his features clearly, but he has dark hair and a dark mustache, his skin is smooth, and he looks kind and handsome from what she's able to observe. He smiles at her and his teeth reflect the low light.

"Good evening, Miss." His voice is velvet with an attractive accent, perhaps English or Scottish, she would need to hear him speak more to determine which.

"What are you doing up here? Are you a prisoner?"

"Aye. I'm afraid so. Where did you come from, then?" Definitely Scottish she surmises.

"I was in the shower and then the ceiling hatch opened. It tried to leave the room, but the door and window wouldn't open. How long have you been here?"

"That I don't rightly know. It feels like a very long time. What is your name?"

"I'm Rail, Rail Ripley. My husband is below with our children. I'm trying to find a way out."

"Ah, I don't believe I will be able to do the same." He lifts his hands and shows her the metal cuffs around his wrists, attached to the heavy chains in the wall.

"What's your name?" she asks, thinking she'll report his circumstances to the authorities.

"I'm Dr. Neill. I'm a physician, mostly obstetrics. I came here to visit a woman and then I woke up in this room."

"You're in the attic of an inn. It's a messed-up place. We've been stuck here since yesterday."

"What do you mean stuck?"

"Our car was towed, and we haven't been able to get any help. We keep being trapped in different places. It's going to sound crazy, it's happening to me, and I think it's insane, but there's this cursed table and when you spin it, you have to kill whoever it lands on, or you'll be trapped."

"Who did your spin land on? I assume you spun it since you're trapped."

"My daughter landed on a female serial killer, named Sarah Janet Robinson, and my husband landed on Ed Gein, another serial killer. My son got H.H. Holmes, and even our dog got one, Ted Bundy. I landed on a falsely confessed Jack the Ripper killer, Thomas Neill Cream. It's illogical, I know, but my daughter and husband were attacked by their targets. I'm sorry I don't know why I'm telling you all of this."

"It's quite alright, Mrs. Ripley. Women find me easy to talk to, perhaps because I'm a doctor. What is it you're supposed to do, with this target?" the doctor asks, shifting his chains.

"We're supposed to kill them to be set free, but I'm no killer. Oh, could that be why you're trapped up here? Did you spin a round, antique table?"

"No. I didn't spin a table. I believe I'm here solely for being who I am."

Her head tilts as she examines the doctor. He smiles softly, bringing a set of dimples to life. She returns his smile but the hair on the back of her neck lifts and a strange chill creeps along her spine. She thinks over the things he's said, and it dawns on her who he must be and she's thankful he's in chains.

"Oh my God! You're Dr. Cream, the serial killer!"

Chuckling he replies with a sparkle in his eye, "My dear woman, I'd begun to believe you daft. Yes, I'm he, Dr. Thomas Neill Cream, accused serial killer. Though I maintain my innocence, I tried to convey knowledge of the true killer to the authorities, but they did not believe me."

"Oh no! You're my spin, you're the one I'm required to kill to be set free." Her head shakes wildly from side to side and tears fill her eyes.

"That is quite the conundrum, however, I don't believe you have a choice in the matter. Perhaps you'd like to free me, and we can work together to escape. I'm willing to form a partnership for our mutual benefit."

"But aren't you supposed to try to kill me?"

"It's what they tell me, but you're not my preference. I've no interest in a wife and mother. Will you consider my offer?"

"How would I help you escape? You're in heavy chains."

"Yes. But there's a key. If you walk towards me and around this other corner, you'll see a door, just next to it is a hook with the key. I believe they placed it within my sight and out of my reach to torture me." She watches him warily. He seems reasonable and not at all like a serial killer. She wants to trust him, but she doesn't want to die. She takes a few steps closer and peers around the next corner. He was telling the truth, she can make out the outline of a door. Obviously, there's a light on beyond the door making it visible in the dark. There's also a hook next to the exit which contains a key.

She navigates toward the door and turns the knob, it twists but doesn't disengage. She pushes against it, and it feels as solid as a wall, there's no give. She removes the key from the hook and holds the cold metal in her palm. There's no keyhole in the door when she checks.

Turning back to the doctor, she weighs her options. She's trapped either in this attic or the bathroom, she's not strong enough to break out. The doctor is tall and appears quite sturdy. If he's willing to help her, maybe she could help him, but she can't let her guard down because he's a killer and could turn against her. But if she doesn't get help, she's going to eventually die trapped in here anyway. Maybe with his help, she can actually get out.

She pats her pocket and feels the reassuring bulge of the knife there. Worse case, if he betrays her, she can still try to stab him. She approaches him again and looks at the chains and how they're secured. A lock connects one end of the chain to his ankle, then the chain loops through a hoop attached to the floor. It goes up to his cuffed wrist where another lock keeps the cuff closed. The chain then goes up through another hoop above him, to his other wrist and ends at his other ankle. Four locks total, keep the cuffs on his limbs secure. The one chain threads through all of the rings, allowing him to move one hand to the detriment of the other.

"If I unlock you, you'll help me break out of here?"

"Yes, Madame, I promise to aid your escape and my own. We will be a team until our release at which point we will each make our escapes on our own. Or in your case, with your family."

"Will you shake on this agreement, giving your word?"

"Most certainly," his smile is wide, and his dimples are deep now. He holds out his hand to seal the deal with Rail. She steps forward and keeps her eyes locked on his, looking for any sign of evil mischief. She puts her hand in his and they shake on their agreement.

After they shake, she uses the key to release his right foot and then his right wrist. She hands him the keys and backs away, allowing him to finish his rescue. She holds the knife in her pocket and watches his every move.

As the chains clang to the floor, he smiles wide at her once more, "There we go. Thank you so very much, Mrs. Ripley. Now let's see about getting us out of here." He turns to the door and takes a running leap at it. When he slams into it, it stops him with a bang, not giving in the least.

"Oh, are you alright?" She moves closer to his collapsed form on the floor.

"Yes, I'm fine, only my pride is injured."

He sits up and then carefully raises to his feet once more. He approached the door and knocked on it, causing a metallic sound to ring out.

"I believe this particular door is made of metal. Perhaps you can show me the way you entered this accursed room?"

"Yeah, it's right around that corner. It's dark over there past the candle."

When he passes the candle, he lifts it to carry it with them, holding it out to project some light in the dark. The opening in the floor allows light from below to project up into the darkness and though it's a narrow beam, it illuminates the space fairly well and definitely better than when Rail first entered, and her eyes weren't yet adjusted to the low light.

He leans over the hole in the floor and looks at the room below. He places a foot on the top rung of the ladder and tests its strength. He turns back to Rail and hands her the candle. She takes it carefully avoiding the hot wax dripping.

"Let me go first and then you can come, that way I can catch you if you slip." He has concern in his eyes, and she feels a rush of appreciation for his consideration.

After he reaches the floor, he calls up to her, "Mrs. Ripley, you may come down."

She places the candle on top of a small chair and then gingerly steps onto the top rung. When she gets turned around to face the ladder she confidently climbs down. When her feet are planted firmly on the floor, she turns to him and smiles her thanks.

He nods and turns to the door, knocking on it to test its make-up, not willing to blindly try the same move as up in the attic. Once he's satisfied, he wrenches the handle trying to twist it open. It moves but the lock doesn't disengage. He bangs on the wood hoping to alert someone at the least. No acknowledgement reaches them through the barrier.

"Did you bring the keys from the attic?" He feels his pocket and removes the key ring. Holding it up to show her, he tries each of the four keys in the lock. Nothing happens though one of them fit perfectly.

"I'm sorry, Mrs. Ripley I believe this is going to be more complicated than I hoped."

"What can we do?"

"Unfortunately, I don't see any other options."

He lunges at her and grips her throat with both hands. It startles her and she doesn't even have time to scream before his tight grip cuts off all sound and breath. Her eyes bulge and she claws at his hands desperately trying to pry them from her delicate neck. She remembers the weapon in her pocket and using one hand to push against

him, she reaches her other hand into the fabric and as she
struggles to untangle the handle from its resting place, her
vision begins to blur at the edges. Her lungs burn with
the desperate need for oxygen. Finally, rescuing the blade
from its bonds, she doesn't hesitate to shove the sharp
implement into her attacker's chest.

As soon as she feels the hilt hit his skin, he releases her,
and she falls to the floor coughing trying to fill her lungs
once again. Her eyes water, the tears flooding her cheeks.
Her breathing is rough and broken with coughing. She
tries to see what happened to her assignment, the handsome doctor with falsely kind eyes. No wonder he was
so successful luring women into his confidence and ad-
ministering poisons to them. They trusted the medication
given by such a good-natured doctor. She shudders at the
thought of all those women.

She sits up and slides her back to rest against the tub.
Her nemesis is bleeding out on the floor, a pool of blood
forming beneath him. His lips are speckled with blood
from his own dying coughs. Rail's eyes are wide as she
watches his breath hitch and then stutter to a stop. She just
killed a man, and she feels strangely triumphant.

"Babe, are you okay? You've been in there a while," Read
calls to her with a knock on the door.

"Read? Can you open the door?" She rasps and breaks
into a coughing fit.

The handle turns and the door opens. He gasps when his eyes land on the pool of blood and the man in the middle of it. His eyes seek his wife and when he spots her, he rushes to her side.

"Oh my God! What happened? Are you alright?"

He cups her face in his hands and looks deep into her eyes. She nods, afraid to speak again for fear of coughing against her raw throat. Poor Rave, she thinks as she realizes this must be how her daughter felt. But even worse, her target choked her for a longer time versus the endless minute of Rail's trauma.

Read kisses her forehead, helps her stand, and leads her to the bedroom where he leans her against the pillows. Rave sees the marks on her mother's neck, and she knows what happened. Without any words she snuggles next to her mom and hopes she's offering support. Randy just watches from where he pets Rogue, trying not to succumb to the fear clenching his chest like a vice.

Chapter Thirteen

The family is subdued, quiet, as they rest and wait for what will happen next. After a few hours, Rogue begins to pace and whine, and Random's stomach is growling. They're going to need to leave the room to allow Rogue out for a walk and much needed relief. Food may be another challenge altogether. Read mulls over the possibilities for food and he comes to a decision.

"We need to take the dog out. We're also going to need some food. I don't want us to separate, but if you want to stay here, I understand, and I'll go alone."

Whispering to protect her bruised throat, Rail responds, "I don't think we should separate either. Let's all go downstairs and walk Rogue, then we can check the kitchen for food. Will you be alright sweetie?"

"I'm okay, and I'm coming with you," Rave answers the question directed at her.

The family loads their pockets with weapons, and everyone carries a backpack, but they leave the tote containing an extra set of clothing for each of them in the room. They carry only the essentials in case they have to make a run for it.

They make it out the back door in the dining room without encountering anyone else, no guests and no staff. The sky is gray, and the sun hangs past the trees in the distance, but the time feels off. Rail felt like she was trapped in the bathroom and attic for three or four hours, but the clock seems to indicate she was only trapped there for thirty minutes. Her mind is having difficulty wrapping around the time difference between the rooms, and the killing, of course.

None of them checked the bathroom after Rail killed the creepy doctor. They were all afraid he'd still be splayed on the floor, but equally afraid he would be gone. None of them voiced their fear and the family was relieved when they escaped the room, being outside is even more freeing. All of them harbor a secret fear of being trapped in a room with a killer again. Random hasn't faced his fear and isn't experienced enough at his young age to imagine the terror of a convicted killer, armed, and set on his end at their hands.

Once the family is outdoors and breathing the fresh, cool air they silently choose to extend their walk past Rogue's needs. A path at the back of the property entices them into the woods where the changing leaves whisper in the breeze. Rogue wags his tail while his nose takes in the fascinating scent of every tree, shrub, and leaf scattered on the rocky trail. The landscape slopes down slightly and as they come around a turn, the sounds of a stream bubbling reach their ears.

As they continue on, a wooden railing frames the way and eventually the ground is made of wood beams, becoming a bridge to cross the stream and it causes Rogue to pause sniffing the ancient oak ground furiously. He's never been on a bridge before, and it makes the jovial pup uncomfortable. He stops in his tracks.

"What's the matter, Rogue?" Rail asks, tugging gently on his leash. He lifts his head, his ears standing up tall, and examines his human. As she tugs again, he leans down, his legs stiff in front of him in defiance and his nose attached to the ground. He won't budge and offers her a whine.

Random kneels down beside the stubborn dog, "What's wrong, boy? Are you afraid of the bridge? I promise it's safe, look." Randy walks in front of Rogue and jumps up and down on the bridge to demonstrate its sturdy structure. Rogue tilts his head trying to understand the lesson.

Rave joins Randy on the bridge and calls to Rogue, "Come on, Rogue. Look, it's okay, we're all going to cross." He takes a tentative step while keeping his nose glued to the ground. His tail wags as he gets closer to the children. When Rail and Read step onto the bridge with him Rogue lifts his head and rushes forward to keep pace with his family. When they reach the center of the bridge, he acts as if he's crossed a thousand bridges and never been afraid once.

When they make it to the other side, Rogue has a new bounce in his step as if he's proud of himself for conquering his fear. But true to form he forgets all about it when a rabbit hops across the path ahead. He takes off running and pulls the leash free from Rail's grasp.

"Rogue! No! Get back here!" she yells after him.

Randy shouts, "Rogue! Heel! Stop! No!"

When the stubborn beast doesn't slow, they all take off after him, slowed by their cumbersome backpacks. When Rogue disappears into the woods, Read removes his pack and drops it on the ground.

"I'll get him, stay here, stay together!" he shouts and chases after the wild creature.

Rail looks around making sure no one is sneaking up on her family, "Don't worry, we'll be alright. Just, um, keep your eyes peeled and be ready with your weapons."

Her head turns continuously watching the woods and the path, trying to keep her children safe. The kids both angle themselves so they can help keep watch in every direction.

Rogue can't resist the scent of the little creature running from him. It's his favorite game, chase. He's slowed by the annoying thing tugging against his shoulders, it's usually held by one of his hoomans and he doesn't mind when they let him know to stop or go by tugging gently, but he hates it pulling on him now. It keeps snagging on things in the forest and stopping his progress, when he really needs to catch that little animal taunting him.

When the leash gets caught on a root and doesn't let him advance any further, he wrestles against it until he's able to slip free from his harness. Completely unfettered he takes off as fast as he can go while still sniffing for the scent of his quarry. He gets close and pounces at the little tease, but it disappears into a hole in the ground. Rogue digs at the hole and barks his frustration, but the animal is lost to him. Even though he can smell its fear and hear its racing heart, he can't reach it. The roots surrounding the den are too strong and they won't budge no matter how hard he digs. Eventually, he gives up and looks around for his family. Not seeing them, he sniffs the breeze seeking the scent of the smallest member of his family, the feet of that one are usually the strongest scent in the house.

When he can't smell anyone familiar, he traces his own trail back the way he came. Before he finds the path to his family, he becomes distracted by the scent of food and snacks. He can smell other hoomans and reasons in his very smart doggy head, his own family may be with the other hoomans. He tracks the odors hoping for a treat and a glimpse of his family. When the cleared path becomes wide, he finds a large container where all of the food smells emanate. But it has a lid preventing him from reaching the snacks inside, he rears up on his hind legs and sniffs at the tiny opening, but he can't reach anything inside. Frustrated, coming up short again, he whines and barks at the container hoping it will dispense some of its treasure.

"Hey, are you hungry? Come're fella, I've got some treats for you buddy."

Rogue looks at the stranger and can smell something delicious drawing him closer for a better sniff. Enjoying the scent and hoping for a taste he approaches the stranger, it's a male taller than his own biggest hooman. Assuming a stranger with treats is a friendly stranger, he sniffs the person's hand and accepts a bite of very delicious meat, almost swallowing it whole.

"Oh, you like hot dogs don't you? Okay, you can have another bite. Come with me, and you can have more."

The stranger approaches a small vehicle, and Rogue pays it no mind, his thoughts are solely on the delicious bites of meat. Whatever they are, those yummy morsels are his new favorite thing in the world. He continues to follow the stranger and when the door opens and the stranger throws several pieces of meat inside, Rogue hops in to gobble them up. The stranger slams the door closed behind him.

Rogue doesn't realize he's trapped inside until the treats are all gone. He sniffs the entire inside perimeter of his prison and when he concludes there's no way out, he barks at the stranger through the window. The stranger meets him at another window and opens the door a small amount wiping the pup's memory of being stuck only moments ago by throwing more hot dog pieces into the back seat. The stranger climbs behind the wheel while Rogue chews up the last bite.

Rogue sniffs the person and gets a whiff of something unpleasant, now that the meat is all gone, there's nothing to cover the scent of death clinging to this person. Rogue remembers that smell from the place with all the barking dogs where his family found him. It was a miserable place with no belly rubs, no treats, no good smells, and no outside. Rogue is leery of the stranger now and not for the first time today, he regrets his decision to follow a tantalizing scent.

"Don't look so sad, buddy. I promise it won't be so bad with me. I'll even give you more hot dogs, doesn't that sound good? What's your name anyway?" The man checks his collar and then scratches his ear, making him feel slightly better about the stranger who stinks of death.

"Rogue, that's a good name. I'm Theo, it's a pleasure to make your acquaintance," Rogue's ears perk at the mention of his name. He watches as the man turns on the vehicle and forces Rogue to sit or tumble off the seat as they move.

They begin to leave the clearing, they turn in front of the path entrance, as Rogue looks longingly at the path to his family, Read rushes from the gap in the wooden fence. He raises his hands in the air, waving them frantically trying to flag Theo down, he shouts Rogue's name which is muffled by the closed windows and the rattle of the engine. Not wanting to lose sight of his family, Rogue moves through the vehicle with his eyes glued to Read as the car moves further away and he stomps on Theo's lap in the process.

Theo loses his friendly voice and shouts at Rogue, hitting him hard and knocking him across the vehicle, "OW! Dumbass dog! Get the fuck off me!"

Rogue's fall into the well beneath the glove box is far from graceful and hurts his hind leg and shoulder, smacking his nose painfully. He shakes his head and sneezes trying to relieve the stinging pain on his snout. His ears press back against his head and the fur on his back visibly raises, he doesn't like the stranger and his lip curls as a low growl rumbles in his chest.

"Fuck you! Stupid dog, now you're a badass? Well too late, I've got you and you're going to be bait for me to find a nice girl to play with, so suck it up buttercup!"

Rogue's head tilts as he desperately tries to understand anything the stranger says but he doesn't recognize any of the words. He thought maybe the man was saying something good, the one sound, play, seemed familiar but he didn't throw a ball or show Rogue his tugging rope so maybe that's not what he said.

Rogue stays on the floor, not wanting to be within reach of the stranger who hits. In his mind he remembers the family he loves telling him, "bad dog!" When Rogue first went to live with them, he chewed on the shoes with the crunchy bottoms. Rogue decides this man's name is Bad Dog, because he did something he shouldn't, just like when Rogue chewed on the shoes. Feeling sad that his family is back in the park, and he's stuck with Bad Dog, he rests his chin on the seat and watches Bad Dog carefully staying on high alert in case he decides to hurt him again.

He thinks about the kind little one with stinky feet who has a warm bed and snuggles him all night, the grumpy one who sneaks him bites of food under the table, the soft one who gives the best scratches with sharp nails and the kind words she showers over him during the scratches. Remembering the biggest member of his family, the one who walks him the most and plays chase, throw, and tug with him, he sighs.

Bad Dog continues to make the car move and Rogue's stomach begins to feel a little bit bubbly. He lets out a burp and licks his lips trying to keep his stomach from revolting. Deciding it might be sitting on the floor upsetting his stomach he climbs onto the seat and looks out the window. Trees zip by and they make him feel dizzy, he tries to focus on the posts in the railing along the side of the road but that just makes his stomach swirl. He stands shaking in the seat and his stomach begins to make that terrible sound warning him vomit is coming, freezing in position with stiff legs as his insides try to force out everything in his tummy.

"No! You better not fucking puke in my car! Mother fucker!" Bad Dog shouts at him but it's too late and everything he's eaten today, including the chunks of meat, comes spewing out of him. It splatters across the seat and between the seats on all of the car parts there and even hits Bad Dog's leg.

Panic forces Bad Dog to jump away from Rogue and as he does, the car jolts, skidding across the road and knocking Rogue into the door. His vomit, pooled on the seat sloshed across his paws and splashes onto the floor and the gear between the seats again. Before Rogue can bolt away from the seat, he's taken over once again by his stomach revolting. He's frozen in the position his body requires as the terrible sound begins again.

In response to another round of dog vomit, Bad Dog scrambles around in his seat, turning the wheel and sending the car careening out of control. The car skids in the other direction and one of the tires catches in the soft dirt on the shoulder of the road. When the front tire sticks in the ground, the speed the car had been going forces it to roll over.

"Mother fuuuuuu...!" Bad Dog screams as the little car flips over and over. He is wearing a leash that keeps him pinned in his seat behind the wheel, but Rogue is loose and is lifted and thrown about his body coming into hard contact with the roof, the door, and the dashboard. He fights to get to the back of the car, he hopes it will be safer there and as he scrambles between the seats he is thrown into the back and he cowers, trying to hang on to the seat despite his lack of opposable thumbs, digging his claws into the vinyl seats. When the car flips over a cliff, Rogue is momentarily airborne, and his eyes are wide as he sees the fast-approaching rocky ground through the front windshield.

Using his paws to brace against the backs of the front seats he hangs on the best he can as the car lands nose first on the hard ground. Rogue is jolted between the seats and his back end meets the ground as it smashes into the car crushing the front of it like a soda can. When the movement stops, Rogue gasps in a breath and assesses his body for injuries. His hind leg is twisted at an odd angle after it got stuck on something when he was being thrown around and his snout stings with a gash, but otherwise he doesn't feel any other injuries.

Rogue pulls himself upright which is difficult because the car is on its roof and up is down while down is up and he's disoriented. He sniffs Bad Dog and listens for a heartbeat, it's faint and slow, he's not breathing and while Rogue listens, the sound of his heart stops. Rogue doesn't feel bad, he was cruel despite his access to tasty chunks of meat. Rogue wants to go home with his family, he doesn't care that Bad Dog is as dead as his scent.

Read makes it back to the family and explains Rogue was taken by the man in the pale-yellow Volkswagen Bug they met before at the waterfall trail. He's sad and hates the fallen faces of his family when they hear his news.

"We'll find him. We just need to get out of here. Come on, let's head back to the inn. We were safe there, in our room and they have food and a bathroom. Maybe we can find a way to use the phone and get help."

"I wasn't safe in the bathroom," Rail remarks.

Feeling deflated, Read agrees, "You're right. From now on, the bathroom door stays cracked open, and we stay together at all times. After we get some rest, we can try walking to the highway. Maybe we can get close enough to signal someone from the highway, it's only a few miles away. Let's rest in our room, repack supplies and head out the moment the sky begins to glow with dawn's light."

"All right. Are you doing, okay?" Rail agrees with the plan, seeing no other way in her tired mind and asks the status of the kids.

"Yeah. I'm fine," Rave answers softly.

"Me too, I just want to find Rogue. I can't sleep without him."

"Don't worry, he's our top priority. Since we know the car, I think we'll find him quickly."

The family trudges back to the inn, no longer happy to be outside. Their collective spirit is sad and broken, beaten down, and defeated. When the blue roof becomes visible through the trees, Read fills with trepidation, he's painfully aware Random hasn't encountered his assignment yet. They climb the stairs and open the front door to enter the lobby.

Chapter Fourteen

When they approach the front check-in desk, the man they can't remember appears as if he was standing there all along. The family speeds up, not wanting to engage with anyone, hoping to make it safely to the room as fast as possible.

"Oh, hello, Ripley's. I requested the manager see you and he's waiting for you in the dining room. Please, right this way." The forgettable man gestures toward the arched entry into the dining room.

"You know what, we're fine. We don't need to speak with him any longer. Thank you anyway." Rail tries to skirt past him. He reaches out and grasps her forearm, stopping her. The rest of the family stops, and the tension is palpable.

"That may be, but he needs to speak with you. I must insist you join him in the dining room." A stern look mars the man's forgotten face, and the family looks to Read for direction.

"Sure, let's put our packs here on this sofa and then we can meet with him," Read says, removing his own backpack. The family follows his lead and shrugs off their packs, all of them setting the bags on an antique sofa. Rail nudges Randy and shows him the knife from her pocket. He nods and pats his front pockets indicating he is armed too. Rave nods at her mother when Rail's eyes shift to her.

The family steels themselves for whatever may be in the dining room. They follow the unknown clerk into the Victorian room, the largest table is occupied by a man with a hat and a mustache. The table is covered with bowls and platters of delicious looking food. There's a bird of some sort, perhaps a goose. A roasted piglet complete with an apple in its mouth is surrounded by bowls of vegetables, carrots, broccoli, and squash. There's a large bowl of fluffy mashed potatoes and a boat of gravy. A large basket filled with bread, rolls, and biscuits rounds out the lovely spread.

The man stands and removes his hat bowing slightly, "Hello. I'm Henry, it's a pleasure to meet you Ripley family. I'm the manager and I understand you wished to speak with me. I like to have a few dinners for the guests each month, and you are here on the right day. Elvira has outdone herself with this magnificent meal. Please, join me. Have a seat."

Read looks over the food and his mouth waters at the sight of such delicious dishes. He pulls out a chair for Rail and uses his eyes to direct the children to seats furthest from the manager.

"Thank you. This looks amazing, we'd be happy to join you. I'm Read, this is my wife, Rail. The kids are Rave and Randy." He smiles and gestures to each family member as he names them. He takes a seat and keeps his gaze trained on the manager.

"It's a pleasure to meet all of you, please, help yourselves. We can pass the bowls, and I can distribute the meat if you'll pass your plates." Henry begins by giving each of them a slice of the goose and the ham. Then Read helps himself to the potatoes and begins passing each dish, Rave helps Randy fill his plate.

"This is very generous. We appreciate your hospitality."

"It's my pleasure, I enjoy visiting with the guests when I'm available."

Henry digs into his food and Randy doesn't hesitate, while the others slowly take in polite forkfuls of the culinary delights. Read keeps his eyes on the manager, assessing him and watching his every move.

"What was it you wished to discuss with me?" Henry finally asks.

Read clears his throat, "We wanted to talk about the Deadly-Go-Round."

"Ah, yes. I surmised as much. I believe Elvira explained it to you and warned you, it was your choice to spin."

"Frankly, Henry, I'm not happy with our visit. Why would you keep such a dangerous item in a bed and break-fast where guests can come into contact with it?" Rail accuses with her query.

"I understand your concerns, but I made that table my-self. It stays here in my inn because it's a family heirloom at this point. I do not interfere with guest's choice to spin the Deadly-Go-Round, I don't even have to warn anyone. But Elvira feels the need to explain the consequences, and I allow her that small liberty because she enjoys telling the story."

Pushing her plate away, Rail glares at Henry.

"My wife is concerned for the safety of our children and she herself was attacked in our room. I think you can understand why she's not happy with our circumstances."

"Certainly, I do understand why you're disappointed with the situation. However, you must look at it from my perspective. I'm a doctor who was prevented from practic-ing medicine and this inn, the guests, and that table keep me happy and occupied since I'm no longer able to indulge in my true love, my profession."

Read's eyes narrow on the man, and he recalls the information on the back of Random's chosen target. His lips purse in frustration while watching the man eat joyfully indifferent to his family's plight.

"What's your plan now? Will you attack our child while we watch?"

"Certainly not. Please do not think me so uncouth. I'm a gentleman, and I wouldn't kill a child in front of his parents, I'm not unreasonable," the monster scoffs.

Read discretely removes a knife from his pocket preparing to stop the doctor from harming his only son. When he attempts to leave his seat, he's unable to move and finding himself trapped, he pulls frantically against the arms and legs of the chair.

"Please forgive me, I had to secure you for safety. You'll be freed as soon as it's reasonable to allow it."

Turning his attention to Random, Henry smiles. It's an evil smile, a smile fit for a maniac, Rail gasps and struggles in her seat. She's as stuck as Read and Rave discovers she's also unable to leave her seat.

"Are you going to kill me?" Randy asks matter of factly.

"That depends, can you kill me first?" He speaks so calmly as if he's reading a definition from the internet.

"I'm going to try." Randy puffs out his chest in a show of strength, Read has never been prouder of his child.

"Then come with me."

Random pushes his chair away from the table and stands when Henry stands. He follows the murdering psycho into the kitchen and Rail finds herself unable to speak. She wants to shout after them, beg Henry to spare her only son, tell her little boy she loves him. But no sound leaves her throat, and tears flow silently down her cheeks. Rave and Read experience the same locked lips as Rail and tears flow fast and hard from Rave's haunted eyes. Read keeps from sobbing, but a few tears splash onto his shirt. Fear like this family has never known clutches them in its grasp as they wait for their youngest member's fate.

In the kitchen Randy follows Henry to the Deadly-Go-Round, Henry sits in the seat which leaves his back to the oven. He indicates Randy should be seated in the other chair across from him. The boy sits and waits for Henry to do whatever he has planned. He fondled the handle of the knife in his pocket and wished in his head for help, or a miracle.

"I wanted to come in here before we move on to the next step. Do you recall what Elvira told you when you spun the Deadly-Go-Round?"

"Yes."

"After listening to her story and her warning, did you spin the Deadly-Go-Round?"

Randy considers the order of events from just a few days ago, then answers, "I did."

"Do you think it unfair of me to kill you?"

"I do. It's just a spinning table, even with the story and the warning, it's not clear how dangerous it is to spin. It hardly seems equal or fair to kill for such a simple thing. My sister was almost killed right in front of me because of her spin. Would you want one of your loved ones to suffer that fate?"

"You're a brave young man I must tell you, grown men have sobbed and begged, unable to have a conversation with me, while you sit strong and tall. I'm thoroughly impressed."

"I don't care if you're impressed. I want you to stop doing this to innocent people."

"I see. What if I only did it to guilty people, would you be agreeable then?"

"How would you know if they're guilty?"

"May I share a secret with you?" Henry asks with a twinkle in his eye.

Random swallows hard and says, "Okay."

"Place your hands flat on the table."

"Uh..."

"Don't worry, you can't be chosen again. You only have one spin in your lifetime. Once you're finished, you are free." Randy places his palms on top of the table, despite Henry's claim, he's careful not to spin it, remembering how sensitive it is and how easily it spins.

"Keep your hands pressed to the table no matter what, you'll be safe."

The room begins to rumble, a vibration starts beneath Randy's feet and spreads to the walls and ceiling. Eventually, the entire room shudders as if there's an earthquake. As he watches, the floor beneath Randy's feet begins to fall away, it breaks apart in large chunks and they crumble and fall into the pit below. An angry red glow becomes brighter as more of the floor falls away. Heat washes over him and an awful stench, like rotten eggs and death, wafts across his nose. He scrunched his face at the smell, his eyes wide as he watched flames reach up from the abyss. He moves his leg to keep from being burned, but he can't move far enough and the flames lick at his shoes and jeans. He's not burned, but the heat is close to unbearable.

"I have very powerful friends. I know who's naughty or nice because I'm told from a very reliable source."

"Santa?" Random asks not sure why he's being sarcastic and poking a snake.

"Close. Try swapping around a few of those letters." When Randy's eyes grow impossibly wide, Henry laughs, enjoying his fear.

"Answer my question. Would you accept the terms of the Deadly-Go-Round if it only worked for the guilty?"

"I suppose so."

"Brilliant!" The floor instantly returns to its normally solid state and Randy blinks as the temperature returns to normal and the stench begins to fade.

"So, from now on you'll only use it on the guilty?" he asks hopefully.

"No. Not from now on, it's always been that way."

"But...my family spun the Deadly-Go-Round and their spins chose a target. My family has never done anything wrong, never harmed anyone. It shouldn't have worked for them."

"Are you sure about that?"

Stunned disbelief mars Randy's face when he turns to stare at Henry with his mouth hanging open. He tries to think of anything his family has ever done to warrant the Deadly-Go-Round spins. He doesn't know if it's possible his parents did something terrible before he was born, but they've been excellent parents and he's positive they've done nothing evil since his birth, making it incredibly unlikely they did anything before his birth. After all, a leopard doesn't change his spots. It's a saying his mother has used when explaining the importance of choosing his friends wisely.

"I'm sure. My parents and my sister are good. Even Rogue, our dog, he's just a sweet, innocent dog. What could he have possibly done to cause a spin to work for him?" Randy challenges.

"He's a tough one. But he actually did commit a murder hard as that may be to believe. The sweet little old lady who had him before you was tripped and knocked down the stairs by your innocent pup. She died."

"He's just a dog, it was an accident if that happened. Dogs aren't capable of plotting a murder."

"Do you believe in souls?"

Thinking it over for a moment, he answers, "Yes."

"Even if a creature should be innocent, it doesn't mean they are, in his case he's guilty of murdering his former owner and his soul is a dark, evil thing, much like my own. He holds the soul of a murderer, and his actions may seem innocent and random, but they're not."

"I don't know why I should believe you, I don't exactly trust you."

"With good reason. But you can't trust him either, he has a way of causing distraction while looking like a goofy sweet dog. If you keep him near you, he'll eventually show his true colors and by then it might be too late."

"What about me? I haven't ever hurt anyone. Why was I able to spin it?"

"Are you sure you want to know?"

Without hesitation he answers, "Tell me."

"Do you remember when you were eight and you were at the lake with your family?"

Random can picture the platform floating in the middle of the lake and the big slide on the dock. It was a really fun trip they took with two other families, and he learned to dive that summer.

"Yes."

"Do you recall the fireworks you stole from the neighbors?"

He gasps a breath in, "How do you know about that?" Shock makes his eyes go wide.

"Do I need to drop the floor again?"

"No. Go on."

"You hid your stolen fireworks in the closet of the kid's bedroom. You never lit the fireworks, but you left them there with the matches. Nobody noticed them until a six-year-old found them the last week of the summer. He decided to light them when most of his family was down by the lake. His father was drunk and passed out on the couch, and he lit those quiet fireworks, they were the kind that light up the sky with a soft crackle. The cabin went up in flames killing him, his father, and his uncle when he tried to save them. Your crime murdered three innocent people."

Gulping for breath with tears streaming down his face, Random looked away from Henry's judging eyes. He was a murderer. He stole those dangerous things and left them where a kid could find them.

"I... I don't know what to say. I didn't know. I didn't mean to harm anyone, doesn't that count for something?"

"Take that to a court of law and see how many years they give you for an accidental murder of three people."

"How many people did you kill?" Random accused.

"I was convicted for nine murders, but they have no clue the true number. Since my childhood, I've killed at every opportunity. Do you know how easy it is to kill people when they're trusting? How easy it is to get people to trust a child or a doctor? I killed two-hundred-forty-four people. Most of them women. I like to suffocate my victims. Do you know what that means?"

"Yes. You make it so they can't breathe."

"Exactly."

"Is that what you're going to do to me?"

"No." Before either of them can say another word, Rogue comes limping into the room. The blood on his snout is dried and his back leg is hanging at an odd angle and he's unable to put it down or step on it. His fur is matted with something crusty and some burrs.

"Rogue! Oh my God, what happened?"

"Oh yeah, he killed Ted Bundy. He was his target, and he didn't hesitate to take him out."

Scratching behind his ear, Randy looks over the dog and worries about the condition of his leg. It looks broken like the bone is completely snapped in half the way it hangs there.

Randy leaves his seat and gets on the floor to have a better look at his dog. He pulls the sharp burrs from his legs and chest making a pile of them on the floor, while assessing the damage.

Rogue seems like his happy goofy self; his injury must be numb. When Randy touches his snout, Rogue holds still hoping for some snacks and relief from his pain. He's able to ignore it until he tries to move it.

"He needs emergency care. What are the chances we can postpone our thing until after we get him to a vet?"

"Unfortunately, I can't allow that. You'll need to do what must be done to earn your freedom." Random considers Henry's words, all of his words, and he decides how he's going to handle what's coming next.

Randy convinces Rogue to lie in the corner and the poor beast whimpers when he lies down but is fine once he's in position. The broken dog rests his chin on his folded paws. Randy slips the knife into his palm and takes a steadying breath.

Henry approaches and holds out his hand offering to give him a hand up. Random uses the kind gesture to make his move and he thrusts the blade upward into the man leaning over him. The substantial and very sharp knife punctures under his chin, almost severs his tongue, and lodges in the roof of his mouth. Blood pours from his wounds choking him, his eyes roll into his skull, and he falls in front of Randy.

Random observes the body of the man splayed before him and seeing he's not dead yet, he stands and removes a large cleaver from a hook on the wall. He doesn't hesitate and hacks into the spasming neck of the manager. His blood spurts in an arc from his severed jugular and paints the front of the commercial oven red. The word Viking drips blood to the linoleum floor.

Randy hears footsteps rushing into the room and already knows it's his family. He drops the bloody butcher's knife and turns to face them.

"Oh! Thank goodness. Are you alright?"

"I'm fine. We need to get Rogue to a vet, he's hurt." They end their joyful embrace, and all of their attention focuses on the injured dog. Read lifts him as gently as he can, and they work together to get him into the car parked outside. Unsure who it belongs to; they're relieved to find the keys in it. Without concern for any of their belongings, they leave Hangman's Bluff the town, and the inn, behind and speed to an emergency animal hospital two counties over.

Epilogue

The twins watch the old woman closely then Anderson asks, "What is it?"

"That... is a Deadly-Go-Round," the cook answers cryptically.

"What's a Deadly-Go-Round?"

"It's like a roulette wheel. It spins and then it stops on a photo with your assignment. It's an antique. It was here when the owner bought the place, so we don't know much about it beyond what it's called and how it spins."

"Who are these people in the photos?"

"Those are criminals, murderers, serial killers, the worst of the worst. Pretty much anyone you land on will be guaranteed to be the scariest monster you'd never want to meet."

"Why do they spin? What do you mean, your assignment?"

"Legend has it, if you spin the Deadly-Go-Round whoever it stops on becomes your assignment to kill. If you don't kill them, you can't leave town and eventually they'll kill you, if you don't kill them first."

With a mischievous glint in his eye, Trayden grasps the edge of the table and spins it. It goes much faster than he expected, and he's delighted. It makes a strange rattling sound, and the noise disturbs Anderson, increasing his anxiety as he waits for it to stop.

When the table slows and comes to a halt, Trayden smiles, "Okay, it landed on..." he lifts the photograph of a fairly young man and reads from the back of the card.

"R.R. Ripley aka The Random Reaper aka Random Read Ripley, Born November 14, 1997, captured May 6, 2020, murdered in prison, August 16, 2024. Convicted of murdering 18 young women, suspected of using a cleaver and hacking up 42+ victim's total."

"Whoa, sick! Okay, it's my turn." Anderson gleefully clutches the table and with all his strength spins the photograph decorated edge. The rattling sound rings out again as they wait for the table to come to a stop once more.

Trayden watches the faces go by in a blur until it finally begins to slow. A woman's face lines up with Anderson's arrow. He flips the picture up onto the table so he can read the back.

"Elvira Bender of The Bloody Benders known as the 'She-devil', arrested October 31, 1889, died in prison 1924? Method: a hammer to the head, more than 20 victims, total unknown."

Both twins turn to the woman standing at the stove cooking more pancakes, "Hey...this looks just like you."

The End

More from E.N. Chanting

Thanks so much for reading. PLEASE LEAVE A REVIEW ON AMAZON AND GOODREADS OR WHEREVER YOU PURCHASED THIS BOOK. THANK YOU!

Books and Series
Forces of Nature Series: Interconnected world of stand-alones
Force of Corruption Book 1
Force Majeure Book 2
Force of Attraction Book 3 (Coming Fall 2025)

Violet's Tales Duet (and A half)

Origin of Violet a novella Book .5 (Free download for newsletter subscribers)

www.enchantingauthor.com

VioleNt Book 1

Vile Book 2

Stand Alone Novels and Short Stories

Haunted Hunting Camp- Horror

The Devil's Affair- Romantic Suspense

Deadly-Go-Round- Horror

The Profit- (Coming soon?)

Southern Suns MC Series: Interconnected world of standalones

Ax- Book 1 (Coming soon?)

Author Bio

E.N. Chanting writes spicy romantic suspense and horror. She lives on the central Florida coast with her high school sweetheart husband and three goofy Australian Shepherds. Her inspiration for writing came after receiving a Mother's Day gift from her daughter. It was a mother/daughter journal where they would each share memories and pass it back and forth between them. When E.N. began to write in the journal she realized she had more stories to tell and wrote Force of Corruption and Haunted Hunting Camp simultaneously over the course of a month.

You can keep up to date with in-person signing events and frequent giveaways by subscribing to her newsletter at www.enchantingauthor.com (You'll get a free download of Origin of Violet, when you subscribe)

www.ingramcontent.com/pod-product-compliance
Lightning Source LLC
Chambersburg PA
CBHW051826170626
46807CB00003B/1045